Prior to Her Death

Kathy Bullingham

Copyright © Kathy Bullingham 2018
All rights reserved

DEDICATION

To my dear husband, all our family and friends.

Acknowledgments

I would like to thank the following
People who have helped to shape this novel into what
it has become.

Georgina Edge; Peter James; Heidi McCall; Mathew
Bridle; Rebecca Seymour; Joe Bullingham;
Sandra Robertson; Steve Robertson;
Brendon Glynn; Sandra Hardman; Louise Hardman;
Georgie Campsey; Chloe Bond:

Prior to her Death

Kathy Bullingham

Prologue.

Friday 30th August 1996

It served as a safe place to hide but it wasn't easy for Suwan, even though she was slight in build. Somehow, she'd managed to squeeze her size eight body behind the chiffonier and into the recess that she had made earlier. It was her safe place where she kept her treasured belongings and savings, ready for her escape to freedom with her beloved daughter. All she needed now were their passports, not that she intended to return to her native Chin – well, not yet. Besides, these were locked away somewhere - probably in her husband's study, just one more place for her to search in this rambling house she once called home.

It had been difficult for Suwan to move this large piece of furniture on her own, not much but just enough. Cleverly, she disguised the gap by using part of the chimney alcove and some tall plants which she had strategically placed. Only *she* would attend to them and keep them watered.

The dust irritated her eyes and as she wiped them with the back of her hand she had to stifle a sneeze, not an easy feat in such poky conditions. In the distance she could hear him talking on his mobile phone probably to his new tart. In a panic, this prompted her to switch off her own before he came downstairs, as to ring now would lead him straight to her secret hidey-hole. She quickly moved her leg to access her trouser pocket; it meant poking her foot out momentarily as she struggled to retrieve it. Then she pressed the phone off. For a moment she closed her eyes, listening to him rampaging through the house trying to find her, which only went to fuel his anger. She could tell he was upstairs in their bedroom because she heard the creaking of the loose floor boards as he moved about overhead. This gave her time to shift her weight and try to collect her thoughts, after all he'd soon calm down.

She wasn't sure if Chiwen had gone out to her friends and couldn't remember what was arranged but just hoped that was the case. It was terrifying for a girl of twelve to witness such aggression from her father, of all people.

Somewhere upstairs, she could hear a small voice, it was Chiwen. He boomed at her to get back in her room. It was clear that he was descending the stairs, each footstep got louder and then silence. Suwan imagined him standing on the bottom step and straining his ears for the slightest noise. She remained very still, barely breathing, hoping he would just go.

He opened the front door and with it a fresh breeze raced in and found her. It was a refreshing feeling on her face and the fragrance it carried, she thought must have come from the pomander on top of the chiffonier, rustling the forest of plant leaves with each draught. Her fear conjured up thoughts of him standing nearby and that when she looked up, he would be peering down at her with his brown unruly hair hanging over his freckled face. But as yet there was nothing apart from the gentle movement of the fronds of the aspidistra. Her heart skipped a beat as she rested her head back against the chimney breast and closed her eyes.

It seemed as if the door had been open for ages, the breeze had become stronger and in its wake fluttered some papers on the table, Suwan visualised them spreading out into a fan shape. She was certain that another gust would ensure their fate - falling to the floor. Then he would come in to pick them up, notice the gap and his dark green eyes would meet hers, catching her out, in her hiding place. She knew these imaginings were borne out of fear, now she could hear him up and down the stairs, carrying some of his stuff into the porch, ready to leave later. Please, please leave she thought.

At last the front door banged shut, Suwan felt sure he had left the house then, but just in case, she decided to wait just a little longer. It seemed like an eternity, crouched in that spot and now she needed to stretch her legs urgently, as they were becoming numb. She shifted her position enough to waggle her toes and could feel the pins and needles in her feet along with a mild cramp sensation that crept up her calves. She listened, for every noise. Nothing. He was gone. Feeling relief she slowly shifted herself and began to count in Mandarin to the lucky number eight, then she started to crawl from her refuge.

From out of nowhere, he appeared and slammed himself into her knocking her breathless to the floor. She was unable to scream because of what had just happened. This time his foot was his choice of weapon and he laid into her with such fury, she instinctively recoiled into a tight ball but he found a way in, to reach her face, her nose, her ears and her eyes. All she could see was a veil of blood like the red curtains on their wedding day, twelve years ago in Kowloon, Hong Kong.

Suwan remained tightly coiled in a ball, as he dragged her along the floor and down the hall to the wooden sea chest. Her fear was so intense she felt her bowels loosen. Then she soiled herself. It wasn't the first time she had spent a night in that chest, she knew this was where she would stay, locked inside this claustrophobic box, until the next day. The only consolation was that he would never hurt his precious daughter.

*

Chiwen heard the commotion going on downstairs but was far too frightened to leave the sanctuary of her bedroom just in case she saw something horrible. First she put away her felt tip pens, in order of colour, neatly into the plastic case twisting each one precisely so that the maker's inscriptions all faced the front. Then she went over to her new CD player and selected the Spice Girls' new album, put the disc in to play, leaving the volume loud enough to drown out her quarrelling parents. She climbed back onto her bed and laid curled up sucking her thumb and reminiscing about her last school sports day when her parents had chivvied her on shouting encouragement and praising her efforts rather than all this fighting.

She thought she heard her father leaving. Only then did she dare take a peek out of her bedroom window down to a neglected garden and on to a gravelled parking area. She watched him as he leant against his shiny black car. He lit up a cigarette and took a long drag, deep in thought as if in a trance. The exhaled smoke slowly swirled in the air around his head and to this Chiwen found herself wondering if it ever made his eyes water. She hated the smell of smoke on him especially when he would give her a hug.

As he came back towards the house, her young heart missed a beat, anxious at what he would do next. She knew her father's rages - they were short lived. Even so, she sighed with relief when he returned to the car carrying a suitcase, then threw it in to the boot. He made more trips, and then methodically loaded stuff on to the back seat. She recalled the stink of her sick that still lingered made worse when the car windows had been shut on a hot day.

Without a glance back, he got into the driver's seat, started the engine and sped off down the drive way spraying loose gravel as he left. Chiwen pulled open her bedroom door and ran as fast as she could down the stairs in search of her mother, fear propelling her on her way and when she reached the bottom step the scene before her made her stop. It was like someone had been dragged through red paint. She stood still and looked around listening carefully to the sound of the fridge humming, accompanied by the outside noises of magpie's cackling and squawking.

It was the coppery smell of blood that reached her nostrils first and in desperation she shouted out for her mother. There was no answer, no movement. Now frantic Chiwen followed the smeared blood trail along the length of the hall's highly polished wooden floor to the old wooden sea chest. Then her heart sank.

There was not a sound within this part of the house, apart from the noisy sparrows tweeting and squabbling in the creeper on the front porch. She glanced over to their singing and just for a moment she pretended nothing had happened and that her mother was busy in the kitchen preparing a meal. She remembered her birthday party when some of her friends had a sleep over. It brought a smile to Chiwen's face, which now turned to tears that flooded her eyes and flowed freely down her plump pink cheeks. She slowly crouched down by the side of the sea chest and fearing her mother may be dead inside it, she whispered.'Mummy. Mummy?'   No answer. Chiwen, gently tapped the side of the sea chest, then noticing her father had not locked it, opened the lid and peered in to the gloomy darkness. The smell from within made her wince, and then her beloved mother looked up at her, with her face bloated, bloodied and full of fear.

'Mummy, mummy, my poor mummy,' Chiwen cried quietly as she wiped her own snot from her nose with the sleeve of her white school blouse.

Her mother tried to speak, but her swollen mouth made it difficult to articulate. Even so, very slowly she managed to say in her native Mandarin.'Shut the lid Chiwen and go to bed, be safe.' Chiwen understood her mother and shut the lid, but she did not go to bed.

Feeling lonely and desolate, Chiwen became overwhelmed with tiredness and fell asleep on the hard floor, sucking her thumb noisily and dribbling onto the dried blood which had started to stain the white collar of her school blouse.

*

The transporter suddenly pulled out from the slow lane, with just a moment to spare which caused Lee to brake sharply. He waited for an impact from the car behind but luckily for him there was none so he quickly checked his rear view mirror to see if it was safe, pulled out into the fast lane and put his foot down. His thoughts became foggy, mixed with emotions and he suddenly felt the urge to cry. Tears started to prick at his eyes blurring his vision. It was then he decided to turn off into the next service station.

He parked his cherished black Volkswagen Golf GT near to the café then reached for a tissue from an already opened pocket-size packet and blew his nose. He then turned the mirror downward to view his blotchy red face, and hoped his eyes that were slightly swollen could safely pass as hay fever. He leaned back in his seat, took out a cigarette, put it between his dry lips then lit it. Next he reached over to the passenger side floor to unzip a holdall, had a rummage inside, took out a bottle of water and flipped its lid open. He stopped what he was doing for a moment, thinking of Chiwen, his most precious treasure in all the world. One day he would make it up to her. He took a few sips of water and another long drag on his cigarette with his eyes closed visualising her laughing in happier times.

No one knew where he was, only perhaps through signal from his Nokia mobile phone. He could be anywhere in the world. Feeling sick to the stomach, not for what he'd done but for breaking contact with Chiwen, he switched off his phone, took out the sim card and put it in a small pocket of his wallet for safety, then returned it to his holdall.

The sharp pain in his foot was relentless as he slowly walked over to the service facilities, following the aroma of coffee he so needed. The taste revived his senses and as he hobbled back to his car he threw his Nokia mobile phone into the bin.

Now feeling in control of his own destiny he got back into his car and joined the steady stream of traffic northwards.

1

Present Day

Mark Eaton watched as the expensive brown envelope was pushed through his brass letter box and then it fluttered down on to his coconut door mat which had the word, "Welcome" across it. He'd been expecting this letter to arrive today. In fact he had first-hand information that it would. After all, not everyone's good friend is his solicitor too. Slowly Mark bent down to retrieve his only mail and turned it over to read the address on the front: Professor M Eaton, Downton House, Mill Lane, Partridge Green, West Sussex. He looked stereotypical of a professor with his dark wavy hair that always seemed like it needed a cut but he preferred to keep it longish. When he stood straight he was a good six foot but his posture let him down. Too much time hunched over books and computers, he alleged.

He looked at the top right hand corner of the envelope and noticed the company's franking mark and in the opposite corner an embossed logo of the solicitors' firm Byrne, Radcliffe & Lewis. Still holding the envelope in both hands he made his way in to the kitchen, perched himself onto a bar stool, reached over for a paring knife from a wood block, pulled it out and slid the stainless steel blade accurately along the envelope's seal. He replaced the knife carefully back in to its slot and slid off the stool where he stood for a few moments, contemplating his next move. He felt apprehension in the pit of his stomach yet some excitement too and now he needed a stiff drink to calm his nerves. Without further hesitation he left the kitchen and went to his study for his favourite tipple.

The two heavy, stained glass panelled doors that led into this room were kept closed and as he pushed them open he could feel the slight resistance from the thick lush expensive carpet where the doors made a smooth whooshing sound over it. He briskly walked over to the Art Deco Burr Walnut drinks cabinet that had belonged to his late father, selected an Edinburgh crystal cut whisky glass and poured himself a large Glenfiddich, neat. He loved the very sound of its descent into the glass and the aroma made him feel euphoric. This was to be a toast, a celebration to the end of his living nightmare.

Mark returned to the kitchen, clutching his glass tumbler in one hand and under his other arm, he hugged his bottle of whisky. His smart phone pinged a text which he chose to ignore. His eyes were transfixed on the unopened letter that lay on the speck-free black granite work top that reflected the ceiling lights, an effect that was made unbearable by their dazzle when the lights were turned on. He did wonder whether to change over to white granite, just to brighten up the kitchen. With his left foot he pulled out the chromium bar stool that he had sat on earlier, the sound of its legs scraping on the stone tiled floor echoed around the units and empty work tops. Not one utensil or electric device was on display, unlike most homes that flaunt the latest espresso machines, food mixers or equivalent. He sat down heavily on the padded seat of the stool, swishing the liquid in his glass tumbler, took another long swig, just so he could savour its contents, then poured himself another one, an extra-large one.

His phone pinged another message. Again, he ignored it. He picked up the envelope and gently eased out a luxurious piece of paper which had been expertly folded. Its creases were so tight that the paper almost refused to open. He read it, looked up and then smiled from ear to ear. At last he was free from that scheming, threatening and slanderous bitch and he drained the remainder of his glass of scotch in one fell swoop. It was his decree absolute.

When Mark had married Sara two years ago, he thought it was the answer to his lonely bachelor life style. He was a good ten years older than her. The marriage's decline was so gradual that he really hardly noticed the change at first. It was insidious. His solicitor friend David Lewis had placed the divorce as a priority, putting it at the top of his list and he pushed it through as quickly as he could before the solicitors' firm unexpectedly made David redundant. Mark hoped he wouldn't need to resort to any more legal battles, especially as David would not be available. But for this, he was eternally grateful to his best buddy who had nevertheless scolded Mark severely for the break-up, blaming his long time bachelor lifestyle, and reminded him that marriage is a heck of a lot of give and take. But Mark was adamant and disagreed, telling his friend that his wife was a venomous bitch, per se.

The mist had cleared to reveal a typical autumnal day. The rusty brown, red and yellow leaves gently floated from their place of birth to form a carpet on the lawn with their crispy sounds under foot. A robin sung eloquently and earnestly in the holly tree which was already covered in berries.

The pungent and nauseating smell from the earlier fire within the pit was not the usual aroma of logs but of the wedding photos, clothes and handbags that the bitch had left behind. With an armful of her books and magazines, Mark made his way back over to the pit and threw then in, followed by some firelighters. Ash exploded instantly from the impact and he had to cover his face, even though the specs of the residue lay on his hair and jumper. He struck a match and tossed it into the pit then staggered back to the kitchen for a top up of the golden nectar.

Another ping from his phone came, but he was too busy dragging boxes out to the fire. He stopped for a few moments and sat on the cold stone steps which wound their way down to the lawn and he picked up his glass of whisky sipping its contents whilst watching the fire's flames lick around the shrinking and curling magazines.

'Hello and what do you think you're up to?' Sara stood glaring at him with keys in her hand.

'Jesus Christ!' Mark said as he almost fell over. 'What the hell are you doing here?' he croaked.

'I still have the keys to the house, remember?' she replied coldly. 'You didn't answer your texts so here I am, to collect my belongings!'

'Too late!' he slurred.

'Yes,' she said as she looked coolly past him, 'I can see that, and what's in that box?

'Your paper work, nursing stuff.'

'I'll take that box.'

'And I'll have back my keys.'

Sara sifted through the box and selected what she wanted to keep, then took it to her car. She returned hoping to retrieve more items, but found her ex-husband leaning menacingly against the open front door, of the four bedroom, detached 17th century house. She smirked as she approached and made aim to pass him and recoiled at his breath.

'Phew, alcohol! And so early in the day,' she said.

'There's nothing for you in here, unless you want the ashes,' he laughed mockingly and immediately wished he hadn't. The drink had got to him.

'You'll be hearing from my solicitor, regarding this unreasonable behaviour of yours,' she said, 'and of course the destruction of my property will cost you, very much indeed.' She turned and threw the keys into the empty space where her chiffonier once occupied, within the large entrance hall.

Her naturally dark green eyes were cold, like pools of black water... black marcasite that occasionally glistened- they made Mark think only of malice. He felt tired now, because of the drink but he'd had enough of her in his life. Now, because of his so- called, unreasonable behaviour, she would be around a lot longer, causing even more turmoil, thanks to his stupidity. As she walked out to her car she gave a glance around, took a last look, then got into her car. The expression on her face Mark had seen so many times before, and he didn't like it.

As she drove off, he cursed himself for not reading his text messages earlier. He turned to stagger back into his house and he could smell the bonfire smoke, that was carried by the gentle autumn breeze and out over the trees.

2

David knew it would not be easy being married to an NHS manager. Secretly he wished Emily hadn't got the job, at least in her previous post they were able to plan their lives. He knew he could be selfish at times especially as he was the one that they had to plan around, up until his untimely redundancy. This had been a blow for him, as he thought being an experienced solicitor in a reputable law firm, he would find a job straight away. At first he wasn't in any hurry, he felt less stress, it was like being on holiday. Yet his new house-husband role was getting to him. Although he enjoyed the cooking part of it, chauvinistically he felt it was woman's work. The thought had crossed his mind to train as a chef. Perhaps he would meet Nigella Lawson some time, he smiled to himself.

David, now lost in his reverie, suddenly became aware of a build-up of steam in the kitchen. Condensation covered the windows like a dense net curtain and the fog within had moved in response to the cold air that rushed in as the back door burst open. It was Emily, looking tired and harassed yet she managed a smile and in her free hand, held up a bottle of wine. 'Peace offering,' she said out loud.

'Accepted,' David replied, as he drained the potatoes into the sink. 'Dinner's almost ready.' He took the bottle from her and started to search for a corkscrew and spotted her looking over to the hob. He smiled to himself, as he knew she was hungry. She looked up at him as he rummaged in the drawer.

'It's a screw lid, David. Give it here and I'll open it,' Emily said grinning at her busy husband in an apron. Obligingly he passed the bottle to her, then gave the open door a quick kick shut. It was the sound of the glugging wine being poured expertly into the John Lewis tall stemmed glasses that enticed David to sit down and join his wife.

'You're looking tired, Em,' he said, as he twirled the stem of the glass in his hand. He studied her youthful face and thought how pretty she looked with her unruly blonde hair pulled back in a clip. Her brown eyes always had a sparkle. She was his pride and joy. They were both five feet ten inches tall but when she wore her heels he loved the way everyone would watch her walk. It was so sexy.

'I'm not surprised,' she said as she placed the glass of wine down on the work top and rubbed her hands over her face. As she yawned, she took a quick look over to the meal that was about to be served and said, 'I'm starving.'

He poured her another glass of wine which she took happily, and now feeling the effects of alcohol she told him of her day.

'In a nutshell, that new waste-of-space deputy manager, Alan, is off sick again. Migraine. That's twice this month and we're only half way through it,' she took a deep breath then announced she would have to catch up with some work tonight. 'I could do with a cigarette now.' She gave David a sideways glance, then turned to face him. 'Just one, please, I feel so stressed.' David sighed, and gave her an apologetic smile, meaning, *no way*, and she knew there were none in the house. She drummed her fingers on the table for a moment and said. 'It's been six whole weeks since I packed up. It's so unfair.'

'Look if we are to get fit we must follow protocol,' he said in jest, which Emily did not appreciate at that moment.'Also, I'm off for a game of squash later just to prove I can keep to my word.' He patted his slight paunch to prove his point.

Emily glared at him and then said, 'Give it a few weeks, David Lewis and you'll be back at those chocolates.' Now she was in a bad mood as her craving for nicotine increased. There was still Christmas to get through, she thought.

'I do believe you are challenging me to a duel over who will be the first to quit. Is that so?' He refilled his glass and got up to serve dinner. Not another word was spoken as Emily laid the table, ready for their meal and emphasised every move, trying to be positive. This fuelled her determination, not to lose.

Later, Emily watched her husband reverse out of their drive into the narrow lane and as he sped off she sighed a relief. Time alone was a luxury these days, she thought, as she picked up a pile of old newspapers. She headed out to the kitchen and as she opened the back door, a draught stirred up the aroma from their earlier meal which wafted around, and suddenly she felt a pang of guilt for her earlier outburst. The weight in her arms started to slide away from her but she just managed to hug the newspapers close enough and almost at a run, she scooped up the lid of the recycling bin with the end of the pile and dropped them all inside. There was one small piece of paper that caught her eye as it fluttered down to the ground. She stooped to pick it up then realised there was a message on it. She read it aloud, 'Fourteen, phone you at the usual time, take good care of our secret phone one, six, seven.' Emily stood for a few seconds pondering over its contents which had been neatly hand scribed, then with a shake of her head, went back indoors and put the note in the kitchen oddments draw, in case it was important for David. She left a note to remind herself to ask him later.

As David pulled over to a lay-by he thought about what delight he was in for tonight? Then immediately, he felt a sense of betrayal, he could end all this now, but how could he do that at this moment? On second thoughts, why should he? It livened up his dreary life and to be honest, a dreary marriage too. He sat waiting, watching the minutes tick by on his dash digital clock. Three minutes past seven. Six minutes past seven. He still felt quite bloated from the meal earlier and as he had drunk a couple of glasses of wine, he suspected he would be over the limit, if only a tad. Even so he left his window slightly open just enough to let out any fumes. The one good thing this time of year was that the evenings were getting darker and no one would notice him but just in case he took out the atlas and pretended to study it. He did feel a bit of a prat.

He checked the Nokia 1100 mobile phone for about the umpteenth time, to make sure he had it switched on and to make sure there was still a good signal, three bars. When she first gave him the phone, she told him not to use it for any other purpose, it was to be their special contact. But it didn't fare well with his image, having to use a cheap end of the market phone with no touch screen, nor internet. He glanced at his watch then back at his dash clock and then the Nokia. They all tallied to the second. It was now almost eight minutes past seven. Although he admired punctuality, this was ridiculous…she was some sort of control freak and now it troubled him that her call was late.

He was sure no one was parked behind him but he still glanced into his rear view mirror, just in case, and caught his own reflection. For a moment he held eye contact, then looked away back down to the phone and scrolled its address book to only one number. Probably this phone he thought, when suddenly it started to vibrate, followed by the Nokia ring tone. He almost dropped the phone as it was so loud. He thought he must have pressed the volume up high when messing about with it. As usual, there was no caller I. D. on the screen but he knew who it was and quickly answered it just before the second ring. His mouth went dry and his heart was racing.

*

As she slowly opened the drawer to her highly polished chiffonier, she smiled as she studied the five cheap Nokia pay-as-you-go phone boxes within. Two of them still contained new phones and all together they represented the five years it took for her dear mother to die. On each of the three empty boxes there were paintings of a pig, an ox and a dragon, also numbers. They meant something to her and as she lightly touched each one in turn, she stopped at the ox and removed it from its companionable group. She was a methodical and tidy person who paid attention to every detail, she just could not help herself. She found her old iPhone in the same drawer, put in her passcode and pressed the pre-selected phone number. It was answered barely on the second ring. She checked her watch, it was exactly eight minutes past, good.

'Hello?' he said a little hesitant, maybe just in case it was not her.

'Hello,' she replied in a low indefinable tone and then deliberately paused.

'Where are you?' He sounded urgent and she liked that. Instead she ignored his question and said, 'I can't make it tonight, something else has cropped up.' Her new date, she thought.

'How about later this evening?' he said.

'Another time, you naughty boy,' she said seductively, then pressed end and switched her phone off. Carefully, she placed it back next to the boxes, counted to three in Mandarin then closed the drawer.

As she sat down on her soft leather armchair, she picked up her glass of Chablis that had now become warm, but she didn't mind, as she held it up to toast the two photos on the mantelpiece, one of her late mother and the other of herself, holding a letter that confirmed her decree absolute.

3

Alan Clarke remembered the short time he had spent in an operating theatre as a student nurse, and how he had hated the whole experience. It was such a negative place to work with all the dos and don'ts, not to mention the dread of error. In fact that was why it was so stressful because every move had no room for errors. It still vexed him as to how anyone would want to work in that kind of environment? It takes all sorts but now here he was in a completely different capacity, as a manager, and relieved that he had just finished his dreaded induction stint in the operating theatre. It was a requirement for all managers - it didn't matter what grade you were, it was mandatory. He knew after that he would be in his own office, free and away from all that yet he still got anxious whenever he went into an operating theatre.

Although he had only been in the job a short while, the pressure was already getting to him, not helped by his over protective wife, Janie. Her mission in life was to push him to his limits especially where promotion was concerned and since his motor bike accident last year she had become even more smothering. But now he could sit back and enjoy his new role and status as an NHS deputy theatre manager. He thought back to the day of his interview where he was sure he had flunked it and when he got the phone call to say that he was successful and the job was his, he did wonder if they had phoned the correct candidate. Nonetheless it pleased Janie. Anything for a quiet life he thought.

A water dispenser had been placed just outside Alan's office where surgeons and anaesthetists would congregate, supping and talking, which infuriated Alan. Then when he did get time to sit down, the incessant glugging distracted and wound him up even further. It had to be moved and the sooner the better to perhaps the main corridor for all to use, along with a couple of chairs for the surgeons. Now he felt a twinge of a tension headache and not wanting it to develop into a full migraine he pulled out two paracetamol from a blister pack that he kept in his desk drawer. He swallowed them with the ice cold liquid, hoping he could finish the morning shift if the painkillers kicked in.

The beginning of any day in the operating theatres was always a hive of activity, check lists, equipment testing, sorting staff sickness and trying to get the right skill mix. He was rather pleased with himself when he offered to make up the numbers that morning. Due to his position as deputy manager, he got to choose where to work, such as, the theatre with the least patients, a low chance of running late and no chance of scrubbing and he had no intention of making a habit of that.

Alan changed from his mufti clothes into surgical scrubs, and as he strolled into the theatre, he spotted a petite, nurse who was already scrubbed and gowned. She was about to set up a surgical trolley in the adjoining prep room, where two other staff were waiting inside for her. The petit nurse demanded to see the patient's paper work and after reading it and checking the patient information was all correct, she then checked the patient's name bands. She then asked the patient their name and checked that the operation site had been marked with the usual black-arrow, drawn on by the surgeon. Satisfied that all documentation was correct the petite nurse then turned and entered the prep room where the door slowly closed behind her.

The anaesthetist went to work on anaesthetising the patient which only took a few minutes. The anaesthetic nurse stood quietly nearby, holding a noisy suction tube in one hand and a lubricated laryngeal airway in the other as the doctor held the patient's tilted head so that the laryngeal airway could be positioned and its cuff inflated. Once the patient was safely anaesthetised Alan turned to look through the small square window of the prep room into which the petite nurse had disappeared a moment ago. The surgical instruments were being checked as he pushed the door open and entered. This nurse looked disapprovingly at him as he had no mask on, and she suggested for him to go and get one. He felt embarrassed and unprofessional that he had forgotten the golden rule of infection control. He rolled his eyes and pretended to zip his mouth, but she was adamant, whilst the other two masked nurses looked on, amused.

The petite nurse then pushed her surgical trolley out of the prep room and waited patiently for the surgeon to appear. Clearly this trolley was her domain, not even the surgeon was allowed to touch anything on it. All the instruments had been laid out in a precise line with an equal space between, each kidney dish and pot was strategically positioned, with surgical swabs placed in a neat step-like fashion. She kept glancing at the record board on the wall to check the count was correct. Occasionally she issued instructions to her circulating nurse and it was becoming obvious that the other staff didn't like her much. Alan started to feel uncomfortable at the lack of interaction between the staff, sensing a tension he'd not experienced before. The cold breeze from the one-way airflow system flooded over him, across his bare arms and down the back of his loose top that gave him goose bumps and made him shiver.

Nearing the end of the operation the petite nurse demanded a sharps and swab count and turned to the surgeon and said. 'I suppose the usual dressing is ok for you?'

'Show me what it is first,' he said without looking up from his suturing.

'The usual dressing,' she said.

'No, for a change I'll have the other type.'

'Do you realise this opened dressing on my trolley costs the NHS, and now I'll have to throw it away?'

'Yes, so next time, nurse, you will not be so presumptuous,' he said icily, as he put in the last of his sutures.

There was a lot of eye rolling from other members of staff and the anaesthetist groaned. At last the surgeon finished the suturing and stood back to straighten himself as he passed the needle holder back to his scrub nurse. There was a moment of deathly hush and anticipation.

'Everyone stop, the needle is missing!' The nurse bellowed.

'It's on the needle holder, nurse,' the surgeon said irritably.

'It is not!' The nurse retorted.

Then began a meticulous search with the careful removal of surgical drapes from the still sleeping patient. Each swab was checked and the used drapes were scrutinised, contents of the rubbish bag were emptied on to the floor and with another thorough search underway someone shouted that they had found the needle. It had been spotted stuck to the front of the surgeon's operating gown. The surgeon gave a half laugh, more in disbelief, then turned to thank the petite nurse for her vigilance, reminding her that it was, after all, her job to check anyway.

'Don't patronise me,' she said.

For a fleeting moment the surgeon pushed his face up close to the petite nurse's face, giving her a menacing sneer. She drew back and said.

'I will be filling out an incident form, on-line, just as soon as I've cleared up here.' She stuck the needle to a sticky pad, then added, 'and another one for your bullying behaviour.'

The anaesthetist blew out his cheeks and as he looked over to Alan, he shook his head and said, 'Another delay.'

'You saw what happened didn't you?' The petite nurse said to Alan.

'Yes and you dealt with it appropriately as per guide lines, well done,' he said wondering if he too sounded a little patronising.

'Well done?' She sounded incredulous.

'What else would you like me to say, after all it was located and no harm came of it?'

The nurse glared at him for a moment, then lifting her head at a slight tilt she half closed her eyes, as if summing him up, then in a soft controlled voice said.'Ok, whatever you say,' and wobbled her head somewhat, her eyes giving a faint smile. Oriental, thought Alan, as the rest of the staff watched her and said nothing.

Throughout the morning the tension in theatre was palpable not helped by the anaesthetist who grumbled on about staffing levels and how slow the lists had become especially when bringing the patients to the waiting area. Alan wondered if he had any Nurofen left in his drawer.

After such a stressful morning Alan could feel his migraine headache had taken hold. He knew the best remedy for this and it would mean getting away from the theatre environment and reducing his tension by going on one of his long motor bike rides up the M23, where he could open up the throttle along a stretch that just leaves the City of Brighton. On second thoughts maybe he'd cycle instead, on his new Boardman Road Team Carbon bike, as he loved the feeling of the wind in his face, and perhaps he could have a quick pit stop at a pub en route. Except first he would have to let his manager, Emily, know that he was about to go off sick. He imagined her tutting and shaking her head at this news and insist on knowing when he would return and no doubt add that there were deadlines to meet. Such a control freak, he thought and wondered if she was the one who wore the trousers at home. But then, her husband *was* a solicitor and probably often read her the riot act. Alan chuckled to himself at the thought of that.

Emily was obviously sitting next to her phone as it was answered on the first ring. 'Emily Lewis, Theatre manager,' she said with a pause of expectancy.

'Emily, I'm afraid I have the beginning of a migraine and…' She didn't give him the chance to finish his sentence and reeled off some appointments and meetings that were imminent. He felt it was her way of saying, don't you go off sick, there's work to be done.

'There's no need to put me under pressure, Emily. I need to recover from this migraine otherwise it'll get out of control,' he said. He could hear her long sigh. What he really wanted to say to her, was after all, we are supposed to be a caring profession, but he didn't have the guts to say so.

'Okay, does that mean you're going off sick, again?' she asked sarcastically.

'This can happen anytime Emily and yes I'm going off sick.'

'Well, now its twelve thirty lunch time so you'll have a good few hours to recover. Let me know before five pm today if you will be fit enough for work tomorrow,' and then she hung up.

Bitch, he thought.

It didn't take Alan long to reach the Hangleton Manor pub and after securing his cycle he removed his helmet and ruffed up his hair from its flattened state. You never know your luck, he laughed to himself. As it was late afternoon and relatively quiet inside the two bar staff looked bored. He smiled cheerily as he ordered a pint of lager, then he held up his glass, as if in a toast and said, 'thirsty work this cycling.' As there wasn't much response from the other side of the bar he moved away quietly to sit down by the window but facing inwards to the newly lit fire that was roaring away in the inglenook fire place. This was the only illumination in the bar. He rubbed his temples to help ease the tension then took a sip of his lager and listened to the logs crackle and spit their sap. It reminded him of bonfire night.

He felt a certain tranquillity as he became mesmerised by the flames that licked up the chimney and occasionally wafted scented wood smoke around the room. The heat was quite intense at times and he felt his eyes water slightly - or was that the drink, he thought? He turned himself slightly to peer out of the small casement window that framed the late afternoon sun, which was now beginning to set on this fine late October day.

He didn't spot her at first until she moved her legs, to cross them. He knew she was looking at him but because she sat with the blazing fire at her back, she was no more than a silhouette. All he could make out was that she had a stunning pair of legs. He looked down at his drink and played with it occasionally sneaking a glimpse. Curious, he got up leaving his drink on the table and walked over to the specials menu board that was hanging next to her and pretended to read. He felt silly at his pretence, aware that her eyes were on him. How he managed to resist looking at her was beyond him, but he thought it was strange that she said nothing. He returned to his table and watched her out of the corner of his eye.

At last she moved and leant forward to retrieve something under her chair, it was a sports bag of some sort. She rummaged inside it and pulled out a mobile phone and although the screen light was showing it was difficult to see what she was doing. He checked his watch and noted he had been there for almost an hour. Then, as if on cue, she stood collected her sports bag and as she was about to leave turned to Alan, who was now able to see her face, helped by the glow of the fire. She gave him a small seductive wave, he responded with a nod, then she was gone. He couldn't help but feel he had seen her before somewhere. He finished his drink and made his way out to his bike and was surprised that the women was standing next to it. She smiled and said, 'Alan?'

'Yes who are you?' he said slightly taken aback.

'My name is Sara.

'Ok, well you know my name, so where have we met before today?'

'At work,' she said with a surprised look on her face. 'In theatre, you watched me scrub for an operation, only earlier today.'

'Oh. I did?' He looked worried in case she mentioned him being in the pub when he was off sick. Damn it, what could he say without it being a lie, he wondered.

'Yes, don't look so worried, Alan.'

'Why didn't you say something in the pub?'

'It amused me to see you pretending to read the specials board,' she held his gaze and said, 'perhaps you will buy me a drink soon?'

'Well ok, yes, when?'

'Soon, when you're feeling better, Alan.' She lightly touched his hand and walked towards a parked taxi. He watched her go and then he started to worry. Would she say something at work?He had to make up an impressive story that even Janie would believe, just to cover himself. He found his headache clearing and started to look forward to going back to work. Yes, the nurse with the oriental-eyes, he thought.

As he cycled back home he decided it best to have the next day or two off sick. It could look bad if he returned to work too soon, especially now as he'd been spotted by one of his staff.

4

The pong from the dying flowers was nauseating, they reeked right through the house, like boiled cabbage does. Pot plants tended not to do that, they were far more independent and survived a couple of weeks or so if they had been watered well. To Sara it always seemed futile buying bouquets for occasions, because often, such events are followed by a planned time away, even if only for a weekend and then who would be around to appreciate them? Her recent gift, of freesias, were clearly past their sell-by date. She wrinkled her nose as she removed them from the crystal glass vase.

They had been from her friend Janie who had her own florist shop in Lancing and was frequently busy making wreaths and bouquets. Her business suited her easy-going persona. She was approachable, confident and cheery, it seemed, on almost every occasion. Whenever Sara popped in to the shop she would be greeted by an amazing aroma of meadows and forests, rather like a pot pourri effect, but never the stench of cabbage there.

Now with all the windows opened and the strategically placed air diffusers the smell had properly escaped, replaced by a chilly breeze which made Sara shiver. As she pulled the windows shut she noticed it had started to rain hard again. She let out a sigh then plugged in the kettle to make a cup of tea, sat down and opened the Shoreham Herald to see what was on at the Rope Tackle Theatre when she spotted on the opposite page an advert for a three week Windows10 computer course. She hadn't quite got used to Windows 8 with its charms at the side that would easily disappear back into their margin especially after a couple of wines.

She got up from the kitchen chair and went over to her antique writing bureau, a present from her ex-husband, as part of the divorce settlement. It was the type that had a roll top. It looked well cared for, but that was typical of - Sara, she took care of her possessions. No dust or crud could be found between the rolled slats. It was an interesting desk with numerous curious compartments that either had no covers or hidden drawers. It intrigued Sara, on the purpose of each one, and what they had contained during their life.

As she rolled up its lid and switched on a nearby desk lamp she reached inside for her lap top. After all, she needed to read the past reviews of this advertised course and was impressed with its four out of five stars. She wondered if Janie would be interested as she'd said she wanted to update herself, too. It would be good company to go with Janie.

She could use any certificate awarded after the course for her Curriculum Vitae. Although she suspected it would only be a cheap pre-printed download on office paper, it would show her initiative and might just impress her manager, Emily. She could take it round to her house to show it off and kill two birds with one stone by taking David's personal effects back to him. It was time to let him go, and move on to the next opponent. She sniggered at this thought.

She poured hot water on to the tea bag within her bone china tea mug swished it around then took it out and over to the bin, where she carefully dropped the tea bag in. She returned to the fridge, took out the miniature jug that once belonged to her mother and poured milk from it. Then headed back to where her landline was and picked it up from its hub, selected Janie's phone number from the address book and pressed the call symbol. A man answered, it must be Janie's husband Alan, Sara thought.

'Hello, can I help?' asked Alan.

'Hello, is Janie there, it's her friend Sara,' she said.

'Oh yes, right, okay, no I'm afraid she's not home yet. Do you want to leave a message or phone back, say, twenty minutes?'

'Your voice sounds familiar, Alan,' Sara said a little flirtatiously. It went quiet for a few seconds on the other end.

'Well, perhaps I've answered the phone to you at other times or maybe we met somewhere?' he said cautiously.

'I think perhaps we have. Were you in a pub yesterday?'

'Ah,' Alan went quiet for a moment clearly gathering his thoughts then said, 'are you Sara, from work… in theatres…?'

'Yes and how are you today?' she asked in a slightly sardonic tone.

'Um… much better thank you,' he said guardedly, 'please don't mention about me being off and in the pub. Janie gets worried about things,' he said uncomfortably.

'Oh don't worry, Alan, I won't say anything,' then she hung up. Sara stood looking at her reflection in the kitchen window then allowed herself a mischievous smile.

The top drawer of the chiffonier with its ornate handles, was slowly pulled opened by Sara. She had previously put in a sheet of a scented paper under its contents. The fragrance of rose oil wafted out and she savoured its scent just for a moment. Then she closed the drawer and opened the next one down to reveal a box containing a brand new but cheap version of a smart phone. She removed it, closed the drawer and went over to her writing bureau, sat down and using a small knife she started to detach the outer cellophane. Once it was free, she slid the lid off the box.

Nearby in one of the bureau's compartments, a small tray containing acrylic paints and a single, slender, sable haired, artist's brush laid idle within. First she set up the pay-as-you-go phone to her corresponding phone. Although Alan was really number four, which meant death, she decided to temporarily paint the Chinese symbol of five on its front. Once she knew his birth sign and lucky numbers, she would scribe them on, in her neatest calligraphy.

A little later her land line began to ring. She had a feeling it would be her reliable friend Janie.

She always got back whatever the situation, a true friend, something Sara had not experienced in her life, apart from her late Mother and often her aunt Maggie. It was something she admired, loyalty. Sara answered her phone.

'Sara, it's me, sorry so late in phoning back, just so busy today,' Janie said without taking a breath. This always made Sara smile. She imagined her friend's flushed face, no doubt her coat would be half off, en-route to a comfy sofa. She could hear Janie say to someone, tea please. It was probably Alan.

'It's not urgent, just a Windows 10 short course about to start and wondered if you would be interested?' Said Sara.

'Um…err…I bet Alan would be more interested, he needs to learn PowerPoint for his new job…' Janie said and at the same time she called out to Alan to join in the conversation. 'I think Al needs to get an update more than me… I try to avoid computers these days…here, I'll put you on to Al.'

'Oh wait Janie…' she said to her friend's fading voice.

'Ah hello again,' Alan said, 'yes PowerPoint is my weakness…' he started to say, when Sara cut in.

'Oh…actually it's Windows 10, a short course, but I'm happy to teach you PowerPoint.'

'Okay, okay that's fine. When does it start?'

'Wednesday evening at seven pm.'

'Okay fine, shall I pick you up?'

'Yes, Alan, definitely,' she said a little too cheekily, 'and tell Janie I'll see her tomorrow at yoga, and don't forget to bring her mat!'

5

It was a drab scene with the staff sitting around eating their lunch yet Daniel Franks sat down and joined them. No one spoke to him and he felt his presence was more of an intrusion but he was so hungry he really didn't care much. As he tore into his ham and mustard baguette, he looked around casually at each person taking in their interactions, like sharing crisps or making tea and coffee for each other. Eventually someone spoke and asked him, who he was. He gulped down a mouthful of half chewed roll that seemed to have an extra dollop of hot mustard. This caused him to blow out of his mouth, like a fiery dragon. Its slow, burning descent, reached that point just centre of his chest when he allowed himself a cough to force the remainder on its course. Now, feeling quite embarrassed, he looked up with watery eyes and half laughed, at the same time looking around to see who had asked the question. A small nurse leaned forward as if waiting for an answer and again she said,' Who are you?'

'Oh yeah,' Daniel said, still clearing his throat, 'my name is Daniel Franks and I'm a medical sales rep for a German company called, OP-Laden.'

'What does that mean in English?' she asked.

'Um,' he spread his hands with palms facing up and said, 'Surgical-Stores.'

'Sounds like a terrorist organisation,' someone said and the others started to chuckle.

Daniel chose to ignore that remark, he'd heard it so many times before, especially as he had been in Iraq during the war and was still sensitive to its reference. He noticed that some staff smirked at each other as someone else said abruptly, 'Usually reps go to the hospital canteen, this is for staff.' Everyone nodded in unison except for the small nurse.

'Well, my friend Louise said it would be okay, she was going to meet me here but I think her list is still going,' he said, as his face reddened and now he wished he'd waited for her. No one commented - just the odd glance up as they continued to eat with sounds of crunching apples, opening crisp packets and turning pages of daily newspaper or magazines as if indifferent.

Daniel quite liked this new job, not only promoting the latest laser technology but state of the art limb supports, too. He liked demonstrating the new products, even the sceptical surgeons showed interest at seminars and it was an ice breaker when it came to trying out the limb supports. Usually he felt like an outsider, particularly when he wore a suit. But today he actually felt part of the team because he had dressed in theatre scrubs. As he put his hand into one of the pockets he discovered a squishy lump which was a creamy yellow in colour and appeared inanimate - well he hoped it was. He continued to study it and just for a moment he imagined it could actually be a piece of diathermias, burnt tissue. Now repulsed that it could be a piece of human tissue, in disgust he threw it away into a bin.

A strange and unfamiliar odour started to waft out from one of the theatres and into the reception zone where Daniel was working. This space doubled up as a patients' waiting area and Daniel wondered if the patients would experience the same as him, tingling sinuses and watering eyes from the acrid smoke. He just hoped it wouldn't turn in to a fire as he had no idea what would be expected of him.

*

Satisfied with his day's work, Daniel smiled to himself as he recapped on the earlier incident in the staff room, definitely he wouldn't be going back there tomorrow. He clicked the last of the show cases shut and placed them safely in the hospital store room which was already congested with some very strange contraptions. Presumably these were used in different procedures although they looked more like equipment of torture. He couldn't help smiling to himself as he pulled the door closed on it all.

Happy that it was time to go home, he looked up as a door swung shut and spotted the small nurse he'd spoken to earlier in the staff room. She looked stylish, smartly dressed in tight jeggings partly covered by an expensive looking tunic and as she pulled on her trendy coat she draped a scarf fashionably, around her neck. She looked confident and classy and was not aware that he was standing there. He speculated that it was the end of her shift and then wondered if she was part-time, as it was only three o'clock. He followed her out, not deliberately, as he was leaving the hospital anyway but decided he would stop her and introduce himself properly but then pondered as to whether it would be appropriate as it might look like he was chatting her up. Most women get offended about feminist issues these days.

He managed to muster up some courage and called out to her. At first he thought she had not heard him so he quickened his pace. Feeling a little embarrassed he said, 'Excuse me?' She turned round to see who it was and in recognising him gave a beguiling smile as he approached. What a relief he thought.

'Sorry to call out like that but I didn't catch your name earlier in the staff room.

'Oh that's alright, my name is Sara, Sara Eaton,' she said.

'Are you off home?'

'No, I'm off to play tennis, want to join me?' she said in mock jest.

'I think I'll give that one a miss but how about a drink after, if you're not in any hurry?'

'Yes that sounds civilised. Where do you suggest?' she said as she flicked her long, almost black hair back off her shoulder.

Daniel became aware of her deep dark green, almond shaped eyes that stared intensely back at him. He felt he was being appraised and briefly looked away, then stammered, 'I'm. . . I'm new around here, so you choose.'

'Ok, how about the Red Lion just on the Old Shoreham Road near the foot bridge, everyone knows it. Eight pm in the bar?'

*

As Daniel sat in his car he looked out of the window for a moment at the fading sky, deep in thought about his new date, not feeling guilty about it. It wasn't that he was looking for anyone, but company, someone to socialise with. At that moment someone tapped on the passenger side window, it was his friend, Louise.

'Ah! I want a word with you,' he said to her as he lowered the window.

'Oh dear! What have I done?' she said, with a sheepish smile.

'Where were you at lunch time?' he said in mock hurt, 'You left me all on my own with all those loose women!'

'Oh yeah… sorry, had to work through my lunch, staff sickness and all that.' She leant on the side of his Ford Focus and said, 'so now as a result of that I've got off earlier today, much like you,' she quipped.

'So are you hovering for a lift?'

'Well yes please. I had planned lifts all this week with one of our managers but he's gone off sick. Thanks Dan.' She got into the passenger seat and belted herself in then looked at him and said, 'I saw you were talking to Sara. Hot date?'

'Actually not so hot, it's more of a sociable drink, you know, work colleague sort.' He frowned at her, 'I need contact, I miss Liz, you know that, Louise.'

Louise nodded her head, 'Sara's very pretty,' she said, 'but tread carefully with her Dan she's known as the 'fatal attraction at work.' Daniel gave her a quizzical look, he knew Louise too well for that to be just a sweeping statement and it left him slightly on edge, apprehensive, like waiting for an ambush of some sort. He sighed and was about to start the ignition but stopped.

He sat still as if in deep thought which gave Louise a chance to study him. His once black hair had now started to turn white at the temples, he looked distinguished and yet rugged with his five o'clock shadow. She thought fondly of Daniel and knew he was aiming to get back with Liz and believed it was her duty to look out for him. He didn't need involvement with that fatal-attraction and her capabilities.

He continued to sit quietly, his eyes tightly shut and his hands fidgeting in his lap. Louise knew of his past trauma. He had always been a private man so now she became uncomfortable,

Prior to her Death

locked in this moment she was not privilege to, as it appeared he may be having a flash back. The deathly hush and his ashen face made her neck hairs stand on end, it was a little frightening. It felt surreal sitting next to Liz's ex who had endured so much mental suffering and life changing events. The late afternoon sun twinkled, illuminating a lone star off to the East. She wondered if it was a satellite or something and at the same time was conscious of the silence in the car, and alone with a brave soldier.

Daniel's army career had been cut short as a result of an armoured car hitting a land mine in Iraq. He was lucky to have his limbs and his life and was only survivor of eight men. It had been a year since the accident, and recovering slowly from his post-traumatic disorder, from which he knew he would never completely heal. He relied on a particular technique of diversional therapy that the psychologist had taught him, a strategy he found useful. But at this moment he began to feel insignificant, panicky, helpless and low in mood. Physically his mouth had gone dry, his heart raced and sweat started to form on his brow. It had been a long while since he felt like this but sometimes it only needed a trigger like a warning. Like the warning to his now dead sergeant not to take the short cut that led to all his comrades losing their lives. He felt guilty that he had survived. If only…

*

Owen watched at a safe distance, next to his car and noticed that she was carrying her usual sports bag. It was difficult to keep up with her interests and activities probably because there was an element of mystery attached and sometimes her clinically ice cold and detached manner unsettled him. He could see that she was up to something, plotting to suit her own needs and now with the medical rep from earlier.

She had agreed to meet Owen at the Hangleton Manor pub at four pm. Instantly her persona seemed to change and take on a new form, excited and confident. Maybe it was because she had something to do with the damage to his car, as someone had purposely ruined it with paint remover. The police said there was absolutely nothing they could do unless there was proof of criminal damage. How he wished she would just get over it and out of his life. She had become far too clingy and talked as if he was about to leave his wife of eight years. Huh, no way! Then his pager went off, he forgot he was on call tonight, damn it, he thought. Ah let her sit and wait for me.

6

The phone hadn't stopped ringing all morning. Emily was on the verge of screaming her head off but it was her job as manager to delegate, and hopefully in most cases, find a solution to problematic issues, one being her new deputy manager's sickness. She now had to make a choice about which would be the most suitable person to step in as a temp for Alan. She leant back in her swivel chair which, under the right force would give out a loud haunting groan that always brought a smile to her face, but not today, not this morning, instead Emily just stared off ahead in deep thought, quietly and trance-like for a few moments.

She ran her fingers through her hair as if trying to comb it away, it didn't work as it fell back into its natural place. Out of her office window she watched the staff flitting about and wondered who would be suitable to take Alan's place today, tomorrow and who knows, maybe the next day too…

As soon as Louise Brookes arrived for work, she was quickly greeted by Owen Muller, who promptly took her by the arm and led her into the deserted staff room. He was clearly anxious about something and as he spoke she could smell his stale breath. It made her draw back a little.

'Look, Louise, I think I have a problem. Metaphorically speaking, a certain person that I have been seeing on the q. t, is acting in a rather unreasonable manner,' he said.

'Oh and what has this got to do with me?' she said puzzled as she folded her arms.

'Well, nothing as such but I know you are aware of my situation.... you know,' he said with a knowing nod.

'Yes I know who you mean,' she rolled her eyes upwards.

'I told her I wanted to end our liaisons,' he started to pace the floor.

'Sleeping together, you mean.'

'Yes, alright,' he said irritated, 'but it was nearly two weeks ago now and all she does is stare at me and make innuendos, it's so unnerving.'

'So?'

'Well, a few mornings ago, I went out to my car and found the paint was peeling off, someone had thrown paint stripper over one side of it,' he said, 'whilst it was parked outside my house and bearing in mind, it's a good fifty yards up my drive.' At that moment he sat down and hung his head in his hands. He beckoned for Louise to sit opposite him. She started to feel uneasy, under no circumstances was she going to get involved she thought.

'Please would you find out if it was her?' he asked.

'No,' she said emphatically. 'I'm not getting drawn into this Owen, it's your problem, deal with it yourself.' She stood to leave then said, 'You should tell the police, it's criminal damage, you know.'

'Yes, well, I have and they said they'd send someone round but I said I'd go to the local station and make a statement.' He paused. 'Obviously I don't want Laura to know I'm worried about this.'

'Look, find out what she wants…what she is up to…it might just be something easy to resolve, I don't know. But I do know that I don't want to be involved at all, it's not my problem, Owen, sorry.'

'She said she'd pop round to see my wife, for a coffee and a chat!'

'Oh dear... Owen it doesn't look good.'

'I'll bloody well kill her if she does that!'

As Louise made her way out of the staff room, she looked back at Owen, he was staring into space. She could hear staff talking some way off in the near distance and getting louder as they approached the staff room. Oh God, I hope I'm not with him in theatre today, she thought as she closed the door.

The day surgery staff chatted at the desk; some voices were raised in competition with the general cacophony, adding to the noises that signalled some staff members' disgruntlement at being deployed. The atmosphere was charged and it appeared more like a busy railway station, with phones ringing and the receptionist passing on messages from the front desk. Patients were reporting their arrival to the ward as other non-medical staff wandered back and forth wheeling trolleys and pushing heavy housekeeping cages. These structured devices rumbled on hard and squeaky wheels and each dent in the floor seem to accentuate their every move. Nursing staff would look up irritated by this, almost as if wanting someone or something to blame.

Louise stood for a few moments listening to it all and yet feeling quite invisible. It seemed obvious that staff had been given their extra duties for today and suspected it was due to the usual sickness. She hadn't been mentioned in any deployment so she decided to proceed to her usual theatre, hoping that the situation would soon calm down. Now she suspected that Owen would be her Anaesthetist for at least the morning and hopefully… Sara wouldn't be working in their theatre today. God she hated working in an atmosphere and actually disliked Sara anyway. But Louise kept her opinions to herself, she had seen so many others air their views out of context, causing unnecessary friction. She preferred to keep herself to herself after all she wasn't paid to be a manager.

There was always a strange mixed odour within the operating department like old plastic and papery type smells, and if the diathermy was in use, the overpowering stench of burnt flesh would waft around creating another stink. Louise noticed Owen was already in her theatre plugging the anaesthetic machine into pipes hanging above it and turning on the power for its monitors. But as she passed the open door of Emily's office she heard her name called and as she turned immediately spotted Emily sitting in her chair looking quite forlorn. She beckoned for Louise to come in and take a seat just as somewhere within one of the theatres a loud and echoing sound resonated from someone dropping equipment. Louise pushed the door slightly closed to listen to her manager.

Emily's desk was in disarray, papers, envelopes and books were all strewn on top, in a haphazard fashion and each time she moved she wafted her expensive perfume around which Louise appreciated. Louise sat down in a chair opposite Emily who, although well-dressed, had today let her hair hang loose around her face, indicating a rushed morning. It suited her but as she spoke, she kept sliding hair over her head to an almost side parting. It was distracting, then she took a deep breath before she asked Louise to act up as her temporary deputy manager for possibly two days.

Louise sat forward surprised. The expression on her face was as if something incredulous had just happened, which actually, had.'Why, what's happened?' She said as it took a few seconds to sink in.

'Alan is off sick and could be for a couple of days and just to top it off, two other staff phoned in earlier,' Emily said as she pulled a folder out from under a pile of sickness returns.

'Why me, am I qualified enough?'

'Of course you are Louise you have a good manner with people, you're well organised and you always get things done,' Emily went on, 'and don't worry about extra pay for this acting up as I'll deal with that.'

The two sat at the desk discussing the next forty eight hours agenda. It meant taking Louise away from the theatre, effectively creating another problem. But this would be remedied with deploying some staff even though there would be some clashes. Emily suddenly became aware of someone standing in the doorway watching them, it was Sara.

'I was wondering why Louise was in here rather than helping us set up in theatre,' said Sara tersely.

'I've seconded her for a couple of days… and we'll sort out anaesthetic nurse cover.' Emily said

'Well I can sort that out.' said Sara.

'That's no worry of yours.' Emily said irritated.

'What have you seconded Louise to do?'

'It's none of your business Sara, please carry on with the checks. Thank you.'

'Okay Emily…' Sara's smile was almost a smirk. She turned slowly giving Louise a cold stare. Emily shook her head as she left. Louise grimaced.

'The main problem here will be Sara,' Louise gave a sigh as she looked over her shoulder checking Sara had left, 'seems she's not very well liked at all,' she said in a near whisper.

'I really can't put my finger on what is so bad about her,' said Emily, 'for some reason she seems to find socialising difficult,' she said with a sigh as she looked at her deputy temp. There was this palpable silence for a few moments which was only broken when Emily leant back in her swivel chair which let out another loud and excruciating groan. 'I've got to get rid of this chair. It's driving me bloody mad!' Louise smirked at the din, then added, 'Also she seems to relish in others misfortune.' Emily nodded in agreement whilst sifting through desk paper. She read a memo quickly and shoved it in a heap.

'We'll need to deploy some staff obviously,' said Emily who now appeared to be searching for something. Louise watched her boss's search and wondered what was so important.

'All very well said and done… but if she has an issue with someone… then it's a different matter,' said Louise still distracted by the desk search, 'especially as she thrives in exposing anyone's weaknesses.'

'Well just for today and maybe tomorrow, I suggest that no one share or show any misfortunes or weaknesses whilst working with her.'

'Okay then, shall I go to these afternoon meetings then?' Louise said as she studied the agenda.

'Great I'll sort out the staff.' At last Emily stopped searching and pulled out a folder with a smile of relief. 'You can go off to our unit meeting,' she said as she shuffled papers together on her desk. Louise now clutching the folder stood to leave.

As she left the office Sara appeared at the door again. Emily looked up surprised to see her back. 'Is there something you want Sara?'

'No I just came back to see what Louise was doing,' she said caustically.

'I think you should return to theatre and stop worrying about things that don't concern you.'

'Oh but there are things that I worry about that concern me, Emily,' Sara said.

'If you have something to say then please say it now, I'm busy,' she glanced at her watch and said, 'I have ten minutes before an important unit meeting.'

'I don't need ten minutes.'

'Okay then just get to the point,' Emily was irritated.

'Oh another day it can wait,' Sara said as she turned to leave. Emily felt bewildered at her behaviour. She could only think that Sara was up to mischief or perhaps she envied Louise's secondment. As Emily stood to go she glanced around one more time, checking that she had everything. She left, leaving her office door slightly ajar in case the desk phone should ring or that someone may need to use it.

The usual stink from burnt tissue drifted through the corridors and partly into Emily's office. It didn't affect her as she was at a meeting.

Prior to her Death

But as the door was left ajar the disgusting smell was only slight in there. Sara entered the office and walked her fingers slowly along the untidy desk. She shook her head at the ramshackle scene before her. Why can't people keep their areas tidy, she thought, as she sat down in Emily's swivel chair.

She scooted in the chair, nearer to the desk and stared at the paper and rubbish on its surface. Disused paper clips that should be in the desk-tidy provided and pens were scattered under, over and in various places that needed to be collected together to join the section marked pens. There was nothing interesting to see. Ah what's in the drawers she thought?

It seemed to Sara that the bottom drawer would contain larger objects or maybe some yummy chocolates and sweets. She hesitated before she opened it and was surprised to find some unusual items a hair brush full of hair, a make-up bag with greasy looking stains at its opening, hair straighteners and a bottle of expensive perfume, Poison. Um she said to herself as she took it out removed its lid and sniffed the spray before squirting some on her wrist. She put it back in its place next to the make-up bag.

The top drawer was locked but the key dangled in its lock invitingly. How careless, she thought then clicked the key and opened the drawer. She stared down straight at the desk diary then looked up to see if anyone was around, she could always pretend to be talking on the phone. She picked up the diary and opened it up to the recent entry which stated a complaint from MFU department registrar Ms Holloway. "Sara Eaton refused to scrub for her and therefore delayed the list while staff were borrowed from another theatre. " There was a note to speak to Sara re this incident. The next entry was Alan off sick 24-48 hours? Need help with meetings etc. Who?

Clearly it was a works diary with nothing personal written in it. She pushed the diary back in to the draw then sniffed her wrist. She raised her eyebrows in approval and opened the bottom drawer again and took out the perfume then sprayed it on both sides of her neck hoping that any residue would soon be overpowered by the burning tissue from theatre. She replaced it then went back to the top drawer to finish her rummaging. She spotted a mobile phone laying indolently to one side and picked it up. It was switched off and conveniently there was no passcode either so it was easy to access its contents. Rather reckless she thought. It looked like a pay-as-you-go phone with EE and it was Emily's personal phone. She scrolled down to the address book and found David's mobile and home numbers. She checked the time, it was just before two o'clock in the afternoon. She considered giving David a visit after her shift ended as Emily would be home late tonight thanks to Alan, she smiled at that thought. Sara's finger hovered over David's mobile number and wondered what he would be doing alone at home today. She pondered whether she should phone him and do facetime- that would be fun but decided against it and pressed his number instead. He answered.

'Hi darling!' David said happily to his wife's name displayed on his screen.

'Oh that's a lovely greeting,' Sara said quietly.

'Who the bloody hell is this?'

'It's only me,' she whispered.

'You've got Emily's phone...'

'Yes.'

'Then put it back!' He yelled at the phone.

'I only wanted to say, hello,' she paused then went on to say, 'I don't like your wife's attitude towards me at the moment.'

'What are you talking about, Sara?'

'After all I'm a very caring person, I give you lots of care don't I?' she said suggestively.

'What's going on for Christ's sake?'

'You can vouch for me can't you David?' She spoke slowly, seductively and said, 'I think I should go David as you sound so upset.'

'Upset, yes I'm very bloody upset!'

'Did you buy that lovely perfume for your wife? It suits me too.' Then she hung up.

Sara put the mobile phone back in its exact place in the drawer, closed and locked it leaving the key dangling. She got up and sniffed her wrist again and smiled. Then she went back to theatre as her lunch break was now finished. Emily's phone rang a few times, then stopped.

7

No one was in the kitchen to hear the splutter and crackle of hot fat that fussed over the frying pan then burst into flames… bumf. The acrid smell of burning oil followed by thick sooty smoke billowed from the top of the Aga and a pungent whiff of burning preceded the fire alarm's high pitched shrill. Normally this was nothing unusual, as it had been strategically placed near the cooking area and usually a quick wafting of newspapers or such-would like suffice, but not today.

David had forgotten the pan he'd left on the Aga, and sat with his head in his hands feeling desperate and sick with worry. The phone call had turned his life upside down. What would he tell Emily? But then there was no need to go too far ahead after all it may just be a little bit of mischief and nothing might arise from this. Sara was always cold and evasive it was part of her character. Mark had warned him to tread carefully. Now he was beginning to understand why. Shit, what a fool he'd been, so infatuated had he been with her charm.

The alarm brought him out of his reverie. God what is that bloody noise and smell, he said to himself. He jumped up in panic remembering that he had left the frying pan on unattended, and all because of that bloody phone call. He ran to the kitchen, sliding on the hall runner, then trying to right himself but falling forward onto his hands much like an ape. And as he stood, he scrambled into the kitchen to an acrid smoke-filled room that beat him back. His eyes were streaming, his throat hurt like hell as he choked his way to the door to shut it. He then phoned the emergency services. He was shocked, so very shocked as he left the house as instructed by the calm lady on the phone.

David watched as the last of the firefighters closed down the locker on the side of the fire engine. The Crew Manager had already lectured him about leaving frying pans unattended. Needless to say how foolish David felt at what had just happened. He didn't dare say that he was aware of fire safety and that it was because his lover was screwing up his mind and he'd lost concentration just for a moment.

He had to let Emily know about the fire but first he had to clean up as much as possible. The disgusting smell of burnt fat had set him off into a sneezing fit, his eyes watered so much it looked like he'd been crying and that is just how he felt at that moment. The devastation in the kitchen was surreal.

He sat down on the hall stairs and phoned Emily, he smiled wistfully to himself as he that ringtone for him was Happy by Pharrell Williams. He felt a little hysteria creeping in to his mood and put it down to trauma. Both traumas.

What if she doesn't answer he thought?

'Hello David Lewis,' she said cheerfully.

'Hello to you, Emily Lewis,' he said gloomily.

'Oh don't tell me you've burnt the dinner.'

'Worse. I've burnt the kitchen and had to use the fire services.'

'Oh God, that bad eh?' Her cheerful mood now sombre.

'I'm sorry I'm a waste of space…' he said near to tears. There was a pause, he imagine her shocked expression sitting with mouth open in disbelief.

'Oh my god David as long as you're alright, no harm to you? No burns?' She croaked down the phone, 'as long as you're okay that's all that matters… so let's look positive…um, as now we can have a take-away.' She said trying to be upbeat for his sake.

He smiled to himself, it was a typically optimistic answer from Emily. That's what he liked about her.

There was a faint smell of smoke around the house which David hoped would fade with the windows open on this damp November day. It had rained almost non-stop for the last week and more heavy rain had been forecast. It meant less time out walking and more time cooped up alone, a miserable thought. As he opened the bedroom window he looked out at the nearby River Adur that glistened from the house lights. The only down side to living here was when it flooded. It made him shiver.

He loved living in the country, surrounded by fields and trees, it was a haven from his previous job but now he was here all the time, he felt lonely and bored. He sat down heavily on the bed and put his head in his hands, his emotion bubbled over and he sobbed at his failings. Screwing his best friend's ex-wife, guilty of infidelity, jobless and now he'd almost burnt down his house, Jesus Christ what the hell have I become, he shouted but no one could hear him. Suddenly there was the sound of a car on the gravelled driveway. He went over to the window and looked out, it was too early for Emily but then she'd probably got off early. The driver stepped out, stooped to reach inside to the passenger seat then materialised holding a large carrier bag, and huddled over as he walked quite fast against the rain and up to the door where he rang the bell.

David had already made his way down the stairs and opened the door to a strong whiff of cooked food. The man held out two carrier bags of Chinese take-away.

'Sorry it took so long, I'm new and it was hard to find where you lived,' the driver said.

'Oh okay,' David said surprised, 'how much do I owe?'

'Nothing, it's paid for.'

After the driver had gone David carried the food towards the kitchen, smiled to himself and then decided to leave it in the dining room in the food heater until Emily got home.

*

There wasn't much of a queue in the Chinese take-away in Henfield and Emily felt relieved that she was almost home and glad to get off work early. As she was about to turn in to her drive way a car pulled out. She didn't recognise it and assumed it was one of David's long term clients. She pulled up near the front door, as the thought of going in through the kitchen made her shudder. She would need to be partially anaesthetised with alcohol before she ventured there, she considered, then she hauled the two carrier bags out of the car juggling the keys, when the door opened to a forlorn husband who instantly looked puzzled at the take-away.

'I have the take-away you ordered earlier, why more food?' he said.

'What?'

'Someone has just delivered to us.'

'Oh that's who must have pulled out of our drive. Never mind it looks like we have someone else's food, I expect he'll come back to collect,' she laughed.

'I'll phone them as it's from Henfield.'

A bottle of opened Shiraz was already in place on the dining room table and the familiar chink of drinking glasses brought some semblance to David's life. He left Emily dishing out the food from the tinfoil containers and went to sort out the extra food delivery.

'I think your driver delivered to the wrong address, as no one here ordered anything from you,' David said feeling a little bit virtuous.

'Oh yes definitely it was for you and the lady paid in cash, said you had a kitchen fire,' said a man at the take-away.

'That's impossible, no one knew about this fire only my wife and she has just been in to you.'

'Ah yes... I saw her here, Mr. Lewis. I thought that maybe you had company tonight.'

David hung up, his heart racing and anger rising.

It was a quiet meal. Emily could see that David was troubled about something but as it had been a shit day for him she thought this was probably down to the fire. She tucked into her meal and noticed that he wasn't eating much. Even his glass of Shiraz was only half drunk. She leant back in her dining chair and dabbed her mouth with one of the napkins she had bought from John Lewis, last month.

'Come on David drink your wine. Don't you like it?'

'Yes of course I do… it's just that I'm tired from the effect of my hellish day, that's all.'

'I noticed on my call history that…' she started to say. He looked up worried, he felt his mouth go dry.

'… you had phoned me earlier today, in fact strangely, it seems that I had phoned you first.' She got out her phone and scrolled through then showed him the call history. 'I was at a meeting all afternoon and left my phone in the office, locked in my drawer. There's no way I would phone you and it looks like you phoned me back.'

'I expect I phoned you by mistake, sorry.'

'The fire was around three you told me.'

'Yes, more around two, two thirty,' he stammered, 'or maybe a little bit earlier,' he sounded annoyed.

Emily looked perplexed, shrugged her shoulders and put her phone back in her bag. She pushed her dirty plate away on the table and then leant on her elbows, chin in her hands and studied her husband as he collected the dirty plates, then plonked them back down on the table. He looked defeated, tired and uneasy on the brink of tears. Emily got up and went round to him and gave him a hug.

'Come on David, it can all be sorted out. . . needed a new kitchen anyway!'

'Yeah, you're right Em,' and he gave her a kiss on the side of her face as she hung her arms around his neck.

A sooty smell permeated through the open dining room door, followed by a small cloud of tiny black particles of smut that floated around the room, helped by the breeze from the opened windows.

'It's too late to clean up anything now, so I'll nip upstairs and shut the windows. God it's blowing a gale!' David said more cheerful now. Then the Nokia phone started to ring. Shit, he'd forgotten to turn it off, what could he say now, he thought? He looked at Emily, wide eyed then he lied.

'That's Mark's phone, he left it here the other day, forgot to return it to him so I'll leave it in my bag.' He said quickly. 'I think I'll turn in…early tonight, Em,' he stammered, 'exhausted from the day's events, you know?'

*

Mark checked the time, still early, eight in the evening and knowing David he would probably be on his second or third glass of Chablis. He pressed his speed dial and eventually the tired soft voice of Emily's answered.

'Hello. .' she said.

'Emily, is your good man there?'

'Yes but he's sleeping, I'm afraid Mark.'

'Too much of the vino, huh?'

'We had a small kitchen fire earlier today and he's rather pissed off and has now gone to bed.'

'Oh God…not too much damage I hope?' he said genuinely concerned.

'Mostly the ceiling around the cooker has smoke damage, the usual stuff. Um…oh by the way did you give David a spare phone?'

'Possibly, although I can't remember. Why?'

'Oh nothing. Anyway I'll let him know you phoned.' She said then went on to say, 'Oh, do you want to leave a message?'

'It can wait.'

It had rained all night and by the morning light it had stopped even though for just a short while. It allowed the sun to emerge for a brief moment before another dark cloud appeared as if by magic from nowhere and confiscating its warmth and rays. The downpour plunged the almost panoramic, country scenery back into gloom. The river in the lower part of David and Emily's garden had now become a raging torrent.

Emily dried her hair in one of their spare bedrooms, not wanting to disturb David. She could smell the fresh fragrance of the Lush brand hair shampoo, fruity and clean even though she wasn't sure what aroma. As she finished dressing she felt a stab of conscience. Should she take the day off? She had so much to do at work and no one to take command. Although Louise was a reliable and sensible person, it would still be too much for her. David on the other hand would cope very easily today, he didn't need her to stay home.

In the distance somewhere downstairs she could hear that infernal ring of Mark's phone, but she decided to ignore it. It wasn't her concern but somehow it had ended up with David, why she thought? She tip-toed down the stairs and once she reached the bottom step she wrinkled up her nose as she passed the closed kitchen door. Her mouth was dry from not having had her early morning cup of tea, and she cursed herself at her lack of planning, and for not retrieving the kettle, tea bags and milk last night. No way was she going into a smelly fat burnt kitchen after her shower. The thought just made the situation worse but it wouldn't take long to get to work and then she'd have a cup of brew.

Mark's phone rang again and this time Emily decided to check it. She rummaged in David's sports bag, screwing up her nose at the usual male odour of sweat and pulled out the offending phone. Good, no passcode and she scrolled to missed calls: there were some from her work, her office. Standing puzzled, her brain was a whir with questions, when it rang in her hand and she almost dropped it as she tried to answer.

'Hello, who's this?' Emily asked indignantly. The line went dead. She checked the address book and missed calls again. Her office phone number showed. Who was in her office? It meant phoning switch to get put through to her extension, as it wasn't possible to phone direct.

There was movement overhead, it was David making his way to the bathroom, the sound of the toilet seat being lifted and hitting the ceramic cistern with a clunk. It was no use calling up to him at that moment, as the thunderous noise of a jet of water hitting water commenced, not helped by him leaving the door open while he took his early morning piss. He flushed the loo.

'David!' She called out. He appeared bleary eyed looking over the banister, his smile was almost boyish.

'Sorry darling…thought you'd gone to work,' he said.

'No, I'm rather confused David wondered if you could just help me out here, 'she said.

'Okay fire away.'

'Why should someone phone from my office phone, at this time of the morning to Mark's phone?'

David stood still for a moment, speechless, his mouth had gone dry and he felt it difficult to swallow the little spit he had left. He almost choked as he answered in a croaky voice, 'mistake… wrong number. It must be, I'll look in to it.'

'Why do I feel uneasy about all this phone business, David?'

'I'm too tired to discuss this now…I said I'll look in to it,' he snapped.

He listened for her car engine to start up, then the crunch of gravel under the tyres sounded like bubble wrap popping. He looked out of the bedroom window as she drove down their drive, passing the leafless gnarled trees that bordered one side of the drive. He could just make out Emily's indicator blinking, even though there was no need for it especially on going out into the single track lane from their drive. He smiled in amusement at this and it reminded him why he loved her and her quirky ways.

8

The casserole dish was as new as on the day it was bought. After each use it would be put in to soak with a squeeze of Fairy washing up liquid. It's true what the adverts say, hands that do dishes are soft but then it could also be because Marigold gloves are worn each time. Anyone who has gone to the trouble of preparing and cooking an expensive meal expects their guest to arrive on time, if not before and if the casserole is left too long its cleaning can be a very stubborn chore.

Sara stood in her living room by the front facing window looking out to where her little white Volvo car stood on the driveway. Her facial expression was deadly serious. There were two things in her life that she just could not bear, being treated as second best by a man and the other was to be lied to by a man. It was her crusade, to hunt out these despicable types. She thought of her ex-husband, Mark. He shouldn't have spent so long on his research, all he really needed was a live-in housekeeper.

Owen parked his car in a different road each time so that no one would spot his car or notice him, even though the evenings were darker now. He checked his phone screen, 18:45, shit he was forty minutes late. What could he say to her? He was fed up with her controlling charms, and snide remarks, so he decided to tell a white lie. Well, it was partly true, sort of, and it was recent as it had only happened yesterday. He felt a sudden rush of contempt for her after all she wasn't his wife, he thought.

The sunset was already gone due to the dark foreboding clouds. It was a pleasant walk up the clean neat road, with evenly spaced houses with plenty of room to build an extension or garage between each one. But most of the residents had driveways and some had ornamental arches with remnants of climbing plants. Owen juggled his car keys nervously in his jacket pocket.

As he approached Sara's modest, detached 1930s style house he saw her at the window, face like a thunder cloud and no doubt scheming up something just to make him feel guilty. He knew he had two options, one, was to be scolded and two he could just walk away and end this doomed relationship. He only wanted a little extra fun on the side, how many men would turn their noses up at that, he thought? He took a deep breath and chose option two.

He returned back to his car feeling a bit of a coward and like all cowards chose the easy way out and opted to text her, on the phone that she had given him then realised he didn't actually have her number. Clearly she had set up the Nokia phone beforehand. From the start Sara had been adamant that he did not use it for private use and that she would never give out their special number to anyone. A control freak but with nice legs, he chuckled to himself.

He found a pen in the glove compartment then searched through his new black leather hospital case for some spare paper then with pen poised he sat staring out of the window trying to compose a message.

It started to feel little chilly inside his Qashqai and already it was misting up so he pressed on the ignition and selected the air con, as it seemed the only function that cleared the windows swiftly, but to aid it along he opened his window to help with ventilation. The temperature fell a little more but he decided to wait for the mist to go before he turned on the heat. There was a whiff of cigarette smoke from a couple who passed his car, and he thought of the stale odour of smoke he had often smelt on his patients before he anaesthetised them. Then, as if this couple had read his thoughts they turned to look at him Owen looked away quickly.

He made his message short, sweet and to the point. It said: " I only wanted us to be friends and didn't expect it to become so involved. I love Laura too much to carry on with this deceit, sorry. " He read and re read it, a clear crisp end to their affair of six weeks then drove round to her house, double parked, got out and posted the letter through her door. The sense of relief was liberating, he felt wiser even though he'd been a bloody fool. It wasn't that he'd been seeing Sara regularly but it was the disturbing fact that she was planning their future. It became obvious to him, what she wanted him to do and no way was he going to leave his wife Laura and his gorgeous kids for this floosy.

Staff slowly arrived for their early morning shift at the Worthing Surgical Suite, unintentionally creating a variety of smells that percolated around the room, perfumes, musty smoke that clung stiffly to the clothes of the last minute cigarette smokers and that damp mouldy smell of wet coats. The floor now hosted an array of soggy foot prints that had become slightly slippery under foot. Someone had thoughtfully put a wet floor cone in place but it didn't stop the slipping and sliding of staff entering the room.

Owen hung his trendy jacket up to dry, luckily his suit was not too damp but even so he shook his trouser legs to remove any excess rain. In the top pocket of his suit jacket, he carefully displayed an expensive fountain pen, which he had no intention of using. He would use the bog standard hospital pen from one of the staff and hopefully, accidently, acquire it. He ran his fingers through his unruly blonde hair, aware he was a dead ringer and namesake for American actor Owen Wilson and with the smooth talking voice to match.

He turned to remove his car keys from his wet jacket pocket and standing quietly behind him was Sara. It startled him but he managed a small smile. He found that he had become more irritated by her presence these days but didn't show it, well not to her face.

'Hello Owen, I've been meaning to catch up with you, face to face, just to thank you for your nice letter,' she smiled. 'It's okay, I understand.' She spoke quietly, gently brushing her hand on his arm.

'Fine, okay I'm glad you understand.' Owen gave another small smile and left the staff room.

Although it wasn't too difficult in working together after the break up, it actually suited him very well that she was so amicable. But there were the odd moments when she would get just a little too personal and inappropriate, especially when she would flirt with him in front of other staff, too complacent for his liking.

'I do like a little bit of fun, you know what I'm like,' she said in a whisper, 'well you like a bit of fun too, don't you Owen?' This was followed by her mocking smile and as she stared calculatingly into his eyes, he looked away. It made him feel uneasy, very uneasy, like a rabbit trapped down a hole. He knew he couldn't complain, not to anyone, after all it had all been true, once. Yeah, but now just get over it he thought.

Annoyingly it had been going on for some time, although gradually, not enough to be noticed at first but then like a rash it had to be addressed. He wished he could sort it out by himself, but he had never been that computer literate even though he was usually generally good with technology. The new anaesthetic machine for instance, Owen could see others were slightly overwhelmed at first and it was him who coaxed and supervised its trial use.

But now he was beginning to wonder if he'd been hacked as there was no logic in what was happening. He was reasonably sure it wasn't a virus of any sort as usually it affects the contacts in the address book, he knew that at least.

It was mildly amusing at first when he started to receive emails about holidays, travel, two for one cruises, some mild porn sites and so on. He assumed they were either from friends or just some spam and yet he wouldn't put it past Sara to carry out a vendetta - but they were harmless. Some of the sites were interesting though and he wondered whether he should book a family holiday with Laura and the kids. He felt a pang of guilt that he'd not paid enough attention to Laura over the last few weeks. He fantasized the two of them on the beach, both basking in the Mediterranean sun, the smell of the suntan lotion on her skin and later back at the hotel, showering together… he was abruptly brought out of his reverie by the sound of the spare phone in his case. He chose not to answer it then wondered if there would be a voice mail service? It can wait, he had more important things to do. Then curiosity took the better of him and he took the Nokia phone out of his case to check the recent calls or a voice mail from Sara. No caller ID, probably Sara. He switched the phone off and put it back in his hospital case, closed the lid and set the combination lock. He made a mental note to give it back to Sara.

He had spent the good part of the morning deleting and unsubscribing more unwanted emails which had become more political, involving racial hatred and sexism. He sat staring at these sites wondering how far Sara would go with her fury. He reached for his coffee mug, took a sip and grimaced as it was now stone cold. He placed it back down on his desk top and wondered how long ago he had made it? He noticed the filmy skin on its surface, and decided it must have been well over an hour old. He went back to the kitchen and made a fresh one, took a homemade mince pie out of its plastic cake container and then sat down at the table, thinking and flitting through the newspaper. He then had a light bulb moment and remembered the computer technician he knew from the hospital IT department.

The operating theatres in Worthing Hospital seemed consistently under staffed, with lots of sickness and tension between staff, and trying to find time to go on any study days was even more remote. Contacting IT had become a fundamental chore in itself, not a brief and straightforward mission any longer, since computerisation and to get through to any department had become frustrating as hell. Owen sat patiently in the new deputy manager's office surveying the boxes of personal possessions of magazines, mostly motor bikes and expensive looking cycles plus a photo of a woman hugging an old black Labrador, with grey eyebrows. He loved dogs too. The phone started to ring and quickly Owen picked up the receiver.

'Hi it's Owen Muller, Consultant Anaesthetist, you were giving us updates on the new system in theatre?'

'Ah yes, I remember you,' said the IT personnel, 'how can I help you?'

'Well to be honest it's my home PC I'm having some trouble with, I think I've been hacked,' there was a sigh at the other end of the phone, ' and I'm concerned that my address book will be raided and this may well affect my NHS emails.'

'Oh dear, well what sort of firewall do you have?'

'That I do not know…not good with computers I'm afraid.' Owen confessed.

'Have you done a full scan of the computer with your anti-virus protector? Like Norton, McAfee…

'Ah yes I have and all is clear, no probs.'

'Okay. Have you any enemies?'

'Quite possibly.'

'Okay. Try changing your email address.'

'I'd rather not.' Owen said indignantly.

'Then if it continues you'll need to report it to your service provider, it's a form of harassment.' IT said and suggested that Owen should be careful with whom he shares his address with in the future. It was when IT mentioned police involvement that Owen laughed it off. He did wonder if it was Sara, he wouldn't put it past her to act out revenge.

Standing in the door way of the office, was his deputy manager Alan who filled his disposable cup with water from the dispenser just inside the office. Further up the corridor someone was calling for recovery and then came the sound of doors being flung open and hitting the wall-stops with a loud thud. More commotion followed.

The click and clatter of a trolley bed being wheeled out on its vibrating wheels echoed a deafening noise. Owen looked up and was surprised to see Alan standing there.

'Hello,' Owen stood and held out his hand, 'I'm Dr Owen Muller.'

'Nice to meet you, I'm Alan Clarke the deputy manager and this is my office, actually.'

'Apologies, but I was rather desperate to use a phone, just for a moment, privately.'

9

Wallace, the little cocker spaniel, ran outside to greet the visitor and it was well worth his effort. He was stroked, had his chin chucked and then to top it all he received a lovely bone-shaped biscuit. His collar gave his name away and the visitor spoke so softly as if she knew him, Wally Wallace, she kept saying. Laura looked out of the living room window and watched this familiar visitor playing with her dog. It was okay,

Wallace was having fun, she thought as she made her way out side to the gravelled parking area.

'Hello?' Laura said, 'I'm sure I've met you before somewhere, haven't I?'

'Yes, yoga. Also I work with Owen in theatre.' Sara said not looking up and still stroking Wallace.

'Of course well, what can I do for you?'

'It's more of what I can do for you!' Sara said as she went to stand.

'Oh, okay, do you want to come in,' Laura said smiling politely, 'Wallace has taken to you very well as if he knows you…I'll put the kettle on.' As she led the way, Sara followed.

'Thank you.' Sara said still making a fuss of Wallace as she made her way to the kitchen.

'Coffee, Tea?' Laura asked.

'Oh neither, I've popped round to give you this….' And handed Laura a Waitrose carrier bag containing an old brown leather brief case. Laura took it with a quizzical frown on her smooth pretty face. She peered inside and took out the case and looked up at Sara.

'Where did you find this?' Laura said.

'Ah ha… I had it in my bedroom all this time!' Sara said in a playful tone.

'What? Sorry?'

'Don't be my dear, I've brought it back to its rightful owner, say hi to Owen when you see him.' Sara petted Wallace one more time and just as she was about to leave said, 'Wallace was always out on a long walk with you, that's why I hadn't met him before. I think he had remembered my scent,' she smiled, 'dogs are funny like that.' Then she left leaving Laura deliberating the visit, plainly to return Owen's lost property but why not deliver to him at work and why didn't he say she had been here as a colleague? He was always doing some research of some sort and visitors were far from unusual. She didn't want to read too much into it, she was sure it could all be justified as harmless.

Instinctively she shook the case and the movement within suggested metal objects rolling around. It intrigued her. Sara had said that she had found it in her bedroom. Have I missed something, Laura thought? She shook the case again then flicked the leather strap out of the way and peered inside. Owen's Fairport convention tee shirt glared up at her - last year's birthday present. She pulled it out, it had a faint odour of his body, and then she found items that turned her stomach into a full flip that caused her a wave of nausea.

Kathy Bullingham

She tipped the remaining items out onto the kitchen table where the aerosols rolled about independently closely followed by a pair of women's skimpy pants, the disposable razor's sharp edge caught up in their delicate fabric which displayed an Ann Summers label. As she stood alone in her kitchen mouth open and in complete surprise with heart racing she let go of her husband's old heavy case, which he said he'd lost a few weeks ago.

Sara walked off down the drive that she had crept up only a few days ago with the Nitromors paint remover, and wondered now where Owen was today. She knew it was his day off, then thought that perhaps he was on call with that new Accident and Emergency consultant, the arrogant one, who clearly liked to assert himself and probably had a gigantic ego. In fact he reminded her of someone, but not quite sure who, possibly one of Mark's old buddies from the past or perhaps a colleague he had lectured with in Pharmacology at the University of Brighton. Sometimes students would pop around with their theses which irritated Sara, as she became tea girl.

The view across Henfield Common felt tranquil with wildlife, the long coarse grass flowed in the breeze and every so often a sudden movement of a bird or rabbit would catch Sara's eye. She stood watching for a few more minutes then got into her Volvo and drove off down the drive. Meeting Owen briefly as they passed, she gave him a little wave and smile. She would've loved being a fly on their wall just to hear what Laura would say to him. Oh, how much he deserved to be punished.

As soon as Owen entered the kitchen Wallace raced to him but all he could do was push him out of the way. His mood was sombre and to make a fuss over a dog was not what was in his mind. Should he call out to Laura, should he act naturally? His own guilt and fear was pushing up bile into the back of his throat. What the hell was Sara doing here? Or perhaps he was jumping to conclusions, she may well have just parked there to needle him. That was her way, always goading… Owen spotted the empty Waitrose bag on the floor, what was he supposed to read from that? It may have blown on to the floor or perhaps Wallace had pulled it down or someone, friend or family had popped in with something that needed to be carried. He thought for a moment, plus they never shopped at Waitrose, Sara shopped at Waitrose. Shit, where's Laura…?

He made his way to the hall where there was a strong smell of polish from the solid wooden parquet floor that made them both feel proud each time their guests arrived for dinner or just a visit. He thought of his children sliding on a mat from one end to the other of this large space, it brought a smile to his face. But now he felt doom as he listened out for his wife of ten years. Then he saw her. Face red and puffy, her blue eyes lost in her swollen lids. She was standing very still on the top stair, he noticed she was using one of his large handkerchiefs and kept twisting it around her finger by its corner. She was clearly distraught at something. He played on the cautious side, just in case Sara had not been here after all? But Laura spoke first.

'I can't stay here,' she said quietly, 'I'm going home and dad is on his way to help me pack.'

'What's happened, Laura?' he asked, trying to gauge the situation.

'I had a visit from your...your... other woman,' she said, 'this is twice in the last three years... and I want out.'

His legs nearly buckled under him as she said that. He was right, Sara had been here and then his mind raced to what she would have said, and how he should answer Laura without incriminating himself too much. He'd been caught out and yet he was not going to dig an even bigger hole for himself. No justification this time round.

'I'm sorry you had to find out this way, please don't be too hasty Laura, please.' He rubbed the back of his head then ran his fingers through his hair, a habit he had especially when he was overwrought. 'We can work it out, we can, please don't leave, not like this, please.' he pleaded.

'Too late Owen, it's all arranged,' she said, 'I need time to think this all over,' she blurted, as she wiped the snot from her face, ' the children will come with me,' then she turned her back on him and went back upstairs, leaving an emotionally charged atmosphere.

Owen, his anger now fuming into a rage, was livid that Sara would do such a thing. Without a word he stormed out of the house to his car, only he knew where he was going.

He banged on her door with such ferocity he thought he'd broken his fist and split the door at the same time. He shouted through her letter box, no light to be seen, the fragrance of her pomander issued a breezy scent as he let the letter box lid slam shut. He still tried the tall back gate latch, even though he knew she kept it locked, so he climbed the wall to get access to the back of her house. There were no lights on there either and although her car was parked outside, to him, she was clearly hiding somewhere. He peered through the downstairs windows one by one and then the conservatory, but he suspected she was upstairs and most probably watching him through the partially closed slats on her blinds. He had a sudden flash of thought, recalling the film with Michael Douglas and Glenn Close, Fatal Attraction, and now Owen understood how Douglas had been driven to brutality.

He sat down heavily on the concrete step by the back door and held his head in his hands as he sobbed in anger, shouting expletives at no one. The step was cold and wet from the rain. His shuddered breath was a sign of exhaustion. He blew his nose and realised he'd been sitting there for about twenty minutes. His bum had become cold sitting on that step and his thin suit jacket did not offer enough warmth for night time raving. He stopped for a moment and listened - he thought he heard a woman's voice and then for a moment it went dead silent apart from the sound of rain pattering lightly on the conservatory roof. Next came the woman's voice again it wasn't Sara, it must be a neighbour who had called out.

'There's no one in, she's gone out with a friend.' said the voice, and added that the police were on their way.

As quick as he could he stood on the wheelie bin to climb back over the wall. The street light was dazzling after the dark back garden and his eyes felt sore and swollen with all the crying. He thought of Laura and wondered if she had gone yet. In the distance he heard the trusted sirens of the police as they got nearer. Owen fumbled for his car keys and made his way to his car but he was too late. Familiar blue lights flashed out their arrival and now he felt defeated, knowing that he would have to acquiesce, so he waited for the officers. They looked young and their belts were decked out with all sorts of items which jangled as they walked towards him.

'We've had a report of a disturbance at this address, are you visiting here sir?' the first officer asked as he took in Owen's state.

'Yes, I'm afraid it was me. I was trying to attract attention from a former friend but it looks like she is out.'

'You look quite dishevelled have you been drinking, been in a fight?'

'No I bloody well haven't!' The two officers gave each other a quick glance.

'Then can you explain your agitated condition sir?' the first officer asked cautiously.

'Yes I'm very upset, that's my condition!' Owen snapped.

'Is this your car parked in front of this house?'

'Yes.'

'May I see your driver's licence and any other identification?' The other officer was speaking on her radio checking out Owen's car registration. The crackle of the transcript could be heard clearly. Owen was conscious of the local neighbours twitching their curtains each time the blue strobe lights flashed from the police car. The WPC was satisfied that the car had not been stolen and with legal documentation, she nodded an okay to the interviewing officer.

'Whatever grievance you may have with the occupant, it's not for the other residents to listen too. Some are elderly and it's frightening for them,' the officer calmly went on, 'I suggest you get in your car, go home and settle down.'

'Go home to what? The evil bitch that lives in this house,' he prodded a finger at the property, 'has destroyed my life and I want to see her!' Owen shouted, at the same time as he pushed past the interviewing officer, who quickly took a step back.

'I'll warn you again sir that if you don't go home peacefully and calm down, I will have to arrest you.'

'I haven't broken any law!' Owen said, his voice now raised. 'I'll sit in my car and wait for her return, if that's alright with you officer?'

'I advise you to leave and go home, sir. Sort this out another day when you feel calmer.'

'I'll do as I bloody well please,' Owen shouted aggressively with his nose almost in the officer's face The interviewing officer, now pissed off, decided to arrest Owen.

'Right, you're coming down the station.'

'This is none of your business! What am I supposed to have done?'

'A breach of the peace, sir.'

Just at that moment the female police officer pointed to the driving licence then added,

'Doctor.' At that Owen rolled his eyes as he was steered to the back seat of the police car.

*

It started to rain again more heavily. The rain drops appeared larger than normal and bounced off the surfaces, like cascading split peas spilling out everywhere. The window wipers were on maximum and had little effect against this deluge. Alan began fiddling with some dials on the dash but still couldn't find the demister or fan. He glanced over to his passenger and shook his head and then sighed with exasperation.

'I don't usually drive this car in fact, I hate the bloody thing,' he gave a smirk mostly to himself, 'Janie was thrilled when she got this car, a bloody Smart Car of all things.'

He reminisced to himself, his first time as a passenger and wondered if Sara felt the same. You couldn't beat a motor bike, whatever the weather, he thought. He indicated to turn in to her road and hit a flood deeper than he expected, the smart car shuddered and then decided to die, right there in the middle of the flood. He cursed out loud as they sat marooned within Janie's pride and joy.

Alan opened the window and looked down at the water, it looked deep enough to come up to his knees. He knew he couldn't leave the car here and wondered if the AA would come out. Sara remained quiet whilst Alan sorted out the breakdown business, then he phoned Janie.

'I'll phone them but I doubt they'll come out not in this weather,' Janie said.

'Well the car's light enough for me to push,' he looked at Sara, 'I'm sure Sara would steer if I pushed it out.' he said to Janie when Sara came up with an idea.

'You can stay overnight if you need to, I do have two spare en-suite bedrooms.' There was a glint in her eyes as she said this.

Alan nodded an approval and told Janie of the plan.

'Yeah I'll get it back to you before eight tomorrow morning, if it's dried out enough to start,' he added, then ended the call. Sara smiled at the idea of sharing her home with her manager. Perfect, she thought. Between the two of them they managed to push the Smart Car up to outside Sara's house, right behind another lonely abandoned car. Instantly she recognised it to be Owen's.

It had become stuffy and cramped inside the Smart Car. Alan rummaged around for an umbrella and where he had disturbed some packaging, a whiff of pine wafted up to greet him. He caught Sara's eye and they laughed at how wet they were already. As they got out of the car Sara gave a quick glance towards the shadows and from her entrance hall she pretended to look out at the rain, but her prying eyes were sweeping the area for something else. She could feel the spray of wetness from the bouncing rain drops, it felt refreshing. Where is he she thought? She took one more look at his car and realised there was no need to be frightened now that Alan would be staying the night. Yes, she felt safer already.

The sound of the thudding rain on her car's roof was as if it had been parked under a water fall. Rivulets of water frantically gushed down her drive only to divide themselves when they met the defiance of her car's tyres, a small resistance to the persistent deluge. No one walked the street in this weather, except may be Owen.

'You can borrow my dressing gown while I dry your clothes out in my amazing tumble dryer,' she said as she selected two expensive wine glasses from her chiffonier then took a new bottle of Chardonnay from the fridge. As she turned back into the living room she realised that Alan had not moved. I like that she thought.

*

Owen spent a quiet, dry night calming down in a police cell. In the morning he was turned out early with just a caution then a police officer drove him back to where his car was left.

The officer pulled up close behind a Smart Car. Owen started to get out when the officer warned him that he would wait until Owen had driven his car away from the scene. Already emotionally drained from his previous day's ordeal Owen was in no mood for any more confrontation.

He studied the close proximity of the Smart Car, then as he was about to get into his own car he felt he was being watched from half opened blinds in Sara's front bedroom. Owen took a look, his adrenaline started to flow. He was sure it was an outline of a man.

*

Sara turned over in her queen size bed, aware that Alan was standing naked, looking out through the blinds. She pulled open the side of the duvet and patted the empty side for him to come back and as she did this deliberately showed her nakedness too.

'A police car is parked outside and this chap had just got out then got in to that car I parked behind,' Alan said as he started to return to her bed, 'and it looked like Dr Muller, our anaesthetist, especially when he looked up at me,' he continued, 'Maybe I should have given him a wave.'

'It's almost seven thirty you'll be late for Janie.' Sara said.

'Yeah, sorry to have to leave,' he said.

'You're welcome here any time, especially now that we have got to know each other,' she smiled, 'I have a smart phone that I can contact you on, it's a pay-as-you-go phone but has no credit on it, one way, I'm afraid, so I'll phone you or we could just make plans when we are working the same shift?'

'Sounds good to me.'

He bent to kiss her good bye and suddenly felt like a new man, completely. Exciting times ahead he thought.

10

Night started early as the black clouds swirled, heaved and darkened the early afternoon skies. Blinking street lights created a glistening reflection on the steadily rising waters like a ballroom light. It had been raining constantly now for five days. Water laid inches deep on the roads, only to be disturbed by the occasional passing traffic thus triggering off an overflow that would then, cascade down into the already drenched gardens. Then sending ripples in the dark, slapping an eerie resonance against a dense structure somewhere not far off.

As Janie flicked on the light in the living room she thought she heard Alan's motorbike but knowing how tetchy he had become since his minor accident last year, she flicked it off again and instead stood peering out of the window from a gap in the blinds. Feeling rather stupid she backed away, went into the kitchen and opened the freezer to a blast of cold air and took out his favourite frozen meal, a Tesco's Indian. She turned it around in her hands and thought as soon as she heard his bike she'd pop it straight into the microwave. Although she'd cooked this many times before she still re read the instructions, just to make sure they hadn't changed then she placed it down on the work top.

The lateness was beginning to annoy her, she didn't want to be trivial but all she needed was to know he was okay. She picked up her iPhone and checked for messages, none. Her finger hovered over his number, she sighed and decided to check her Facebook news feed, next plan was to phone her friend Sara, as she'd know what to do but her phone went straight into voice mail. Janie chose not to leave a message, infuriated, she pressed end and half threw the phone down to a clatter. It started to ring almost immediately. It was Sara.

'What's up Janie?' she asked.

'Alan's not home yet and I'm getting worried, I wish he'd phone me,' Janie said, 'What would you do Sara, he's been late quite a lot just lately.'

'Oh it's not that late now, Janie, stop fretting. He's probably stuck at work, he is a manager, with NHS meetings…and you said he loved going on long rides on his motor bike.'

'For goodness' sake Sara, it's pouring hard with rain and its flooding or hadn't you noticed?

'Yeah, well, give him another half hour then phone him.'

Janie felt angry, after all, if it had been her late home, he'd be the first to whinge. She sat down heavily on the sofa, switched on the TV and scrolled to the local news for the weather forecast, more rain. What she needed was some feel good factor, sunshine.

As Alan opened the front door, rain splashed in behind him, and Janie could hear him stomp his feet on the door mat. She leant forward to see him through the gap of the door hinge, he was unzipping his leathers. He called out as if it was normal to get home late in gross weather. Didn't it occur to him that she was worried, she thought?

'Hi Janie,' he said chirpily.

She didn't answer.

His leathers were soaked from the ride home and the process of peeling them off would take him some time so he sat down on the bottom stair and got to work on his biker's boots first. He shouted out to Janie again and still no answer.

After a struggle he hung up his wet leathers in the hall to let them dry naturally then went in search of Janie. She was sitting quietly on the sofa looking very serious, her arms crossed and pretending to be watching the news with the volume on low. Alan plonked himself next to her and sensing her anger he started to justify his day.

'It is raining out there you know, lots of puddles and floods.'

'You could have phoned me,' she said sulkily.

'I wish you wouldn't interrogate me like this.'

'This is not an interrogation, it's concern, why couldn't you just phone or text me?'

'Look, I was wet, and it's not easy to use a mobile phone in this weather,' he said defensively.

'You could have phoned me sooner, from work, before you left?' She raised her voice.

'I didn't know I would be this late, anyway I like going on long rides, you know that.'

'You just said yourself, it's raining, loads of puddles and floods. Where the hell do you go?'

'Look I don't need this Janie. I'm tired.'

'I'm tired too trying to run the shop single handed, late deliveries because of the weather which could mean a loss of business and worrying about you!'

He stood up to leave the room, he hated any form of confrontation. As he started towards the hall Janie spoke.

'I phoned Sara,' she said, 'and funny enough she agreed that you like going on long bike rides too. How would she know what you liked?'

Alan glanced at Janie and just for a split second they locked eyes. It was then she realised that something else was going on, female intuition.

'What's happening Al?' she said softly.

'There's nothing to talk about, just that you get so protective at times it's... it's almost suffocating.'

'What's happening Al?'

'It just did…just did…sorry.'

'Sorry?'

He faced her and took a deep breath. Her hair was held up in a clip that she wore when she went for a bath or shower. Rogue strands of long hair escaped it and lounged on her shoulders creating a masterpiece of beauty that had first attracted him to her. He looked away not wanting to have eye contact.

He knew he had to confess his affair or part of it. He'd already thought it through and would tell her the affair had only been that one night he'd stayed over, aided by wine and poor taste. Yes, he was sure that Janie would eventually forgive him, he would promise it would never happen again. Well not promise, he thought. Janie waited for him to speak.

'I had a fling. It's over,' he said not wanting to admit with whom at that moment, he'd do it gradually, let it sink in first. Then get it over with.

'What… with Sara, my friend, you had a fling?'

Alan hadn't said Sara's name but then who else would it have been? He looked away from Janie as he spoke.

'It just happened, that night I stayed when your car got stuck in that flood, she was only a fling, Janie, nothing more than that.'

'Do you expect me to believe it was only that night while you've been getting home late since that time…do you think I'm a fool, Al?' Janie said, her voice now raised as she left the room for upstairs.

The quietness in the house was insular to the sound of heavy rain on the already deepening waters that were once puddles. Janie lay very still on her bed, thinking, planning and knew she had to get out, away from all this. He'd destroyed their happiness, things had spun out of control. She had to leave him, let him sort himself out. Her new determination, the only the consolation for her wounded pride, propelled her decision to go, tonight.

Using the street light for illumination she went out to the landing cupboard where the suitcases were stored, took one out, threw it on the bed, unzipped it in one swoop and started to pack with determination. As she looked up Alan was standing in the doorway, he couldn't have been there for long. It felt spooky in the gloominess with him staring almost indolently whilst she busied herself. Why should she feel fear, was it because her life had left the status quo behind, she thought? Then he spoke.

'Don't leave me,' he pleaded.

'Leave me alone,' she snapped, 'you're a lying bastard.'

'It's late, it's still raining hard and you don't have anywhere to go.'

'Don't I?' She spat her words at him.

'Don't go,' he moved towards her, she withdraw, 'at least let's talk... I don't want her...I'm sorry...you and I have so much to stay together for. Don't we?'

Janie pushed past him.

Her hand bag was open conveniently for her to throw in a few last minute items. She tucked her iPhone into a pocket of her waxed Joules jacket and then slid it on, took one last look around the kitchen and the living room thinking to herself, at least it was a Friday, she'll

have the weekend to simmer and make decisions. The cool air that entered through the opened front door had flapped at the unguarded newspaper on the kitchen table. Janie grabbed her car keys and made for the door.

'For God's sake Janie, where will you go?' He sounded frantic and went to hold her.

'Out of my way...' she screamed. He took a step back, shocked. He'd not seen Janie like this before.

She looked out at the lashing rain then she stepped out onto a flooded path, splashing her way to her Smart Car that already looked as if it was on a small island with water swirling around it. She opened its small boot, heaved her case into the tiny space and slammed it shut.

'Janie, stop, don't go please…please!' He shouted from the front door then moved out towards her as if to stop her from going.

'Leave me alone. . . !' she yelled back at him through the noise of the unrelenting bombardment of rain.

With effort she made her way to the driver's door and pulled it open as the heavy downpour splattered onto her seat within seconds. She started the engine, slammed the door shut and drove off down the road creating a spectacular wash, leaving Alan on his knees in the rain, crying and pleading for her not to go. Too late now for that drama she thought.

11

The rain had been unyielding, even the windscreen wipers struggled to cope under the barrage but the fast and steady beat helped Janie to concentrate. She searched the little side pocket of the driver's door for a tissue and found an old one but as soon as she dabbed her eyes it became soggy in no time. She managed to move the seat belt enough to pull out a small packet of tissues from her jacket pocket. There was a mixed smell within her car of damp pine, it was a new spray from her florist shop that she had been working on and now it would not be finished. Janie worked on her own but as her business grew, occasionally she relied on her friend Sara…she would have to contact…Oh… she had no one to contact for help now…

The demister was blowing on its highest and hardly clearing the condensation that clung to the windows. The sudden sound of a car horn jolted her back to reality, she realised her driving had become erratic not helped by the dazzling lights of the oncoming traffic that reflected in the wetness. She decided to pull into a layby to collect her thoughts and plan her next move. It had been a good thirty minutes since leaving home. Her little car shook and trembled at each passing vehicle leaving a covering on the windows of a thick glue of mud that had been stirred up from the floods.

She kept the car engine idle as she opened the electric window slightly to let in some fresh air, then rested her head back feeling the cold wetness from her jacket's collar which had now become stuck to her skin by the Velcro fastener, it pulled on the tiny hairs on her neck. She calmed herself enough to make a plan and decided that she would go to her parents even though they lived a good three hours away. There was no point in phoning them at the moment. It would only mean that they would worry about her until she had arrived. She took out her smart phone and checked her Facebook wanting to voice her thoughts and share the post, it was so tempting. She felt so pissed off with everything. She pulled open her handbag and rummaged for a dry tissue when her mobile phone vibrated. It was Alan. She chose to ignore it and the constant delivery of texts and missed calls that lit up the car's interior each time. She drove off from the layby to join the manic Friday traffic.

It had been almost three hours since she had left the comfort of her home, her life shattered. She became overwhelmed with misery, a feeling she had not experienced before except when as a child, her cat was hit by a car. She felt similar now to when her mother broke the news to her. She remembered crying herself to sleep that night and the next day her father brought home a kitten. Yes that was the nearest to experiencing misery she'd come, albeit briefly, she thought.

Janie needed a break, to stretch her legs and have a pee. She was desperate as now her belly ached from a full bladder, making her jeans feel two sizes smaller. Not far ahead she spotted some lights just off the road that looked like a little-chef of some sort, and now with her indicator flashing in the dark interior, she drove into the almost deserted car park to join the few parked cars. She got as close to the café as possible noting that the flood water was slowly creeping over the tarmac, emphasised by the sporadic lights that shimmered their reflection, occasionally disturbed by the odd ripple.

Within her hand bag a continual flow of bright flickering light emanated from texts and missed calls. Perhaps it was her self-pity and curiosity that inspired her to read one of them. It said, "Please come home. " Please, huh thought Janie and she quickly switched off the phone not wanting to read anymore. Thanks to his betrayal she was here tired and alone. She pulled down the visor for the vanity mirror and took time to apply a little make-up. She studied her face carefully then automatically gave it a smile of approval. The noise from the relentless rain that drummed hard on the car roof was a testament that she would have to make a mad dash over to the café and once in the dry, click her door locked with her key.

All eyes turned to see who had entered, Janie gave a cursory smile to acknowledge their presence as she walked over to the counter, selecting a sandwich and a mug of tea. She paid in cash then made her way to a lone table partially obscured from the other diners. Here the lighting was of a lower level, more private and although there were only half a dozen people in the café, she chose to sit with her back to them and avoid eye contact.

She took a sip of tea and resumed the task of opening the tightly wrapped cellophane that hugged her sandwich into a high security state. Her thoughts went to her friend's betrayal, wondering if Sara was aware that all she was to Alan was just a fling, a throw away fling.

Someone pushed their chair back on the wooden floor which startled Janie back to reality. She deliberated on checking her phone, and as she sipped her second mug of tea, she rummaged for it in her bag, took it out and yawned. She needed sleep her exhaustion and stress made her feel disoriented, detached. She looked up at the café clock, one o'clock in the morning then switched on her phone. As it fired up, the Apple logo appeared, illuminating her area of the café. She punched in her passcode then the text messages streamed in one after another their alert tone echoed around as she had left it on full volume. She instantly knew, without looking behind her, she had disturbed the group of people so turned to them, and meekly smiled an apology as she quickly fumbled the phone into silent mode.

She started to read the text, the most recent and it said, 'it will be different.' She wondered if he meant, since she had left, or was he considering moving in with Sara or did he intend to go celibate? She began reading Alan's first text, which took ages to scroll for, he had sent so many, all from a desperate repenting man….

'I'm sorry please come home, I love you.'

'Please come home so we can talk about it, I love you.'

'Please come home, I know I've been a shit, sorry.'

'Do you remember when we hiked up Vesuvius and made a promise to each other?'

Yeah, be there for each other whatever forever…yeah I remember, so now I suppose it's my fault, she thought?

The message continued, '…and when we got to the summit we took a selfie together, with the crater in the background, and instead of saying *cheese*, we said, *forever*?'

'It won't happen again, I promise.'

Your promises mean nothing, she thought. As if reading her thoughts the next text read:

'We said through thick-and-thin, ups-and-downs, please come home. Janie, it just happened. I've let you down working too many long hours, we need to catch up. Things have happened so fast recently, new job, just gone to my head, all of it. I drove around aimlessly on my bike, just thinking of what I had become.'

Just for a moment Janie shut her eyes and went straight into a dream. It was the sudden rush of fresh air from the open door that awoke her. God, she thought, is this what it's like when you work nights? She looked at the dead screen on her phone and pressed it back in to life then continued to read.

… it just happened, I regret it, a big mistake. I want you to come home, I'm worried about you in this weather.'

Like I had been worried, about you being late, huh! A taste of your own medicine she said to herself.

'For God's sake Janie come home!'

Janie realised she had been in the café far too long, it was almost two o'clock in the morning. She was overwhelmed by tiredness and emotionally drained. Alan was right I need to go home and talk she thought. She texted him.

'I'm coming home,' she said.

'I'll wait for you,' he texted back.

*

The hot drinks and sandwich had hit the spot but as it would take a good couple of hours travelling back, she bought another sandwich, a bottle of water and some chocolate then left for the car park. The tarmac had all but disappeared under water. This reminded her of paddling in the sea where the waves would wash up around her ankles and the residue would, momentarily, stay at a depth that just covered the foot. She yearned to be back in her home, surrounded by familiarity.

Prior to her Death

Because of the floods, diversion signs appeared to be on just about every road. Janie cursed the satnav as it would be useless against any re-routing. She drove over to a small space on the side of the road to study her map, it was Alan's idea to keep a map in the seat pocket as a back-up. But the shadows created by the weak interior light meant she'd have to use her phone's torch even though the phone's battery was low. She noted there was a short cut through to Salisbury via a small, possibly single tracked road which she hoped would keep her journey to a minimum.

It was a relief to leave the A303 and get onto a network of lanes, now as part of her new route home. She gave a quick check of her phone, no signal, no little bars in the corner of the screen. As there was no service and the battery was less than thirty percent, she switched her phone off, after all she probably wouldn't need it now as she was on her way home.

It was no use, Janie knew she was lost, with no other traffic, no street lights and the relentless rain that bounced off her pug-nosed Smart Car, she wished she had stayed on the A303.

She turned up the radio hoping to hear any weather news, radio heart which played non-stop music was no good for weather updates so she tuned into the local radio frequency but nothing, just talk. She gave an exasperated sigh yet was feeling more upbeat than when she first started out last evening. She opened up the spare sandwich packet, glad she had bought it earlier. It was cheese and onion and it tasted good even though the pungent smell of onions would linger for some time.

There was a sudden drag on the steering as she hit a deep puddle, her heart leapt a beat and she thought she was going to scream. As if by miracle, straight ahead was a sign post, a wooden three way type, she slowed to read it, part of the words were worn away she lowered her window to take a better look. Rain pummelled her face as she could just make out Wilton, straight on. She took another look at her map and decided to drive to this village outside Salisbury.

The unforgivable mist forming on the inside window screen, was distracting Janie from concentrating on driving. She was tired and each time she wiped it away it would come fogging back within seconds. Each breath she took just seemed to add to the condensation problem.

She switched on her phone to check for any messages, none, and still no service symbol so she switched the phone offto save the battery life which was now only 20%. The radio volume was on its highest setting but was still too quiet, competing with the demister's blower. She decided the CD player would better so she put on the 90s CD compilation, which Alan had bought for her last birthday. As she reminisced she realised she should try to phone him and let him know where she was or more to the point where she thought she was. There was another part of her that wanted to play out this drama to the full – possibly self-indulgence to punish him. It now smelt stale and stuffy inside the car so she started to rummage around for some form of freshener. She would have to make do with her lavender Body Shop spray.

*

Every so often Alan would jump awake thinking he heard her car. He took another look out at the early morning deluge and tried her mobile number again. Voicemail was his only communication with her but now her phone stated it was switched off. He shouted out in frustration. 'Oh for fuck's sake Janie, answer the God dam phone!'

He shivered, it was cold and the heating was not due to come on for another hour, at five o'clock.

*

Janie thought about parking in a layby somewhere as she was going round in circles, lost. She would have a nap and wait for it to get lighter then hopefully with less rain she would resume her journey home. Not a bad plan but for the fact she was now in low lying land with no place to stop so she travelled a few hundred metres before she became aware of water both sides of the lane. She slowed her speed from twenty miles an hour to ten, straining her watery tired eyes, through sheer exhaustion.

There was an occasional glint from her car's side lights. She now felt fear and then a moment later she ploughed through what seemed like a small flood with its wash splashing up onto the windscreen. It sparkled in the headlights. But it was too late, her car bobbed slightly then the engine screamed out for something to take purchase on. She felt the sensation of swaying, floating, when the engine cut out and the windows wouldn't open. She wasn't sure if her feet had become cold from the lack of hot air blowing from the heater or if they had become wet. Water seeped further in to the footwell of her car and up on to her lap, slowly making its way upwards and in her terror, her fight for survival took over. The last thing she saw was the empty sandwich wrapper floating past her eyes and the last thing she thought of was Alan.

*

Almost five o'clock. Alan's anxiety had increased to panic level. He paced the floor occasionally and he stood vigil at the window overlooking the area where Janie usually parked her beloved Smart Car. The only consolation was that she was coming home, even though she hadn't replied to his last text or call. He sat down and focussed on possibilities like signal failure perhaps or just maybe she didn't hear it or the phone was left in silent mode. He had endless thoughts on why she was late back. Then he heard the click of the thermostat at five o'clock.

He wished she had said where she was at least he could have gauged how long her journey would take. He closed his eyes for just a moment then woke with a start, his heart pounding in his ears. The room was warmer but he felt a chill deep inside.

Water dripped rhythmically from a blocked gutter and onto the window ledge. He swung his legs off of the sofa, noticing that the room was still partly illuminated from the street lamp. Yawning, he stood, stretched and glanced at the television digital clock, nearly six thirty. He couldn't remember falling asleep, where the hell is she, he thought?

It was just before seven in the morning when Alan picked up his phone from the coffee table. He'd pre-selected his in-law's phone number, and after all she may have stayed with them for the night. He knew phone signals were poor to non-existent in some areas in the West Country, but in spite of that she may have changed her mind about coming home after all. She had her reasons and he was in no position to judge.

He rubbed both his hands over and around his face listening to the sound of his rough dry skin that seemed amplified in the quietness within the house. Decision made, he picked up the phone and pressed the pre-selected number, but after five rings it went into voice mail. Shit.

'Hum…morning it's Alan, is Janie with you? If she is please get her to phone me? Thanks.' He ended the call and went to put the kettle again, his mouth felt parched and he could smell his bad breath, it made him cringe. For the umpteenth time he made a mug of tea but forgot to drink it.

The dark dismal day meant the lights would stay on for longer, it felt unnatural somehow and yet still the winter had only just started. He watched his reflection in the windows as he walked from room to room, pacing and waiting, until the phone rang. It was Janie's mother.

'Hello Alan, no Janie here I'm afraid. Is everything ok?' she said.

'Well, no, everything is not ok. Janie walked out on me last night, we had a row,' then in an almost whisper, 'silly really.'

'Oh no, it'll soon sort itself out, Alan. Have you tried her friend, Sara?'

'Um. . . no she wouldn't be there, thought she'd go to you. She's been gone all night and my last text from her was just before two o'clock this morning,' he said contritely then gave out an exasperated groan.

'I can't think where she would have gone,' she soothed. 'Have you contacted the police, after all they know how to locate phones and phone company stuff, they'll track her down easily, just you see.'

'I'm so tired, it was all my fault…if only…' he muttered.

'Look, Alan, we'll be here all day, phone whenever you want but let us know as soon as she turns up and vice versa. In the meantime we'll put our thinking caps on. She may well be trying the land line so I'll go now.' Janie's mother hung up.

*

Alan watched the police car park just outside his house then two officers got out simultaneously. One a woman the other a man. They walked slowly up to his front door regardless of the unrelenting deluge. They had serious expressions and Alan just knew that it was bad news….

12

The whole forty eight hours had been surreal, it's not something to ever relish, a death,

the death of his wife…he knew what triggered this event and he felt that he had committed manslaughter. Unimaginable amounts of anguish had transported him to a place he had never

in his wildest dreams been to. Not even, not ever, could he have envisaged this outcome, a destiny, Janie's demise.

His numbness kept him busy. In his quiet dishevelled mind, the access to fond memories was so fleeting and each one had prodded his urge to cry out. But it was fleeting, in magnitude. In a way this allowed him to sneak the odd reflection of his own behaviour. His guilt was in remorseful overload and he hoped this would end in his own demise too.

*

When the door opened both Emily and Louise turned their heads, an automatic reaction, like most, when not expecting anyone else to arrive - least of all Alan. Nothing was said, somehow it had become a speechless sensitivity, and the in fact it was out of place for him to be at work at all.

The whole sorry business of dealing with death and associated arrangements were well outside his capabilities, it was always Janie that dealt with that sort of thing. His gratitude did not appear obvious but Emily did not mind, she had seen shock before and grief takes on many forms. She suspected Alan was in complete denial, and that was why he was at work.

Alan found himself babbling on, justifying his presence. He'd arrived to work…what was he supposed to do? Yes… of course he should be at home, mourning Janie there and not in his office. Impulsively he hung his head, because that was what he wanted to do at that moment, it was a reflex action of despair. Emily quickly moved towards Alan, acknowledging his distress. Feeling quite inadequate in this situation, she insisted on taking him home to his relatives and let them take over. After all, he was in no fit state to be rational. He didn't resist instead he allowed Emily to steer him out of the office to drive him back to his family. Louise watched them go.

It was the light tapping on the office door that caused Louise to look up sharply. It was Sara, peering around it. She entered uninvited, sat down on the chair opposite Louise, in Emily's swivel seat, and started to twist slowly from side to side. Then she stopped and looked about the office.

'This office needs a good tidy up, can't imagine how people can tolerate working in such a mess.' Sara said.

'Are you serious?' snapped Louise, 'There's been a death, or hadn't you heard?'

'Yes of course, I'll be going to the funeral,' Sara looked appropriately solemn, 'Janie was my friend too you know!'

'So I hear. Was Alan aware?'

'Yes.'

'Were you friends with… the two of them?' Louise asked in almost disbelief.

'Yes… but in different ways,' Sara smiled and looked away momentarily, then back at Louise, 'so what's your role today Louise?'

'I'm still acting up whilst Alan is on compassionate leave, it's official now or it will be on Emily's return.' Louise stood and said, 'I'm busy right now Sara so I'll let you get back to the theatre.'

'If you need any advice or help just give me a call,' Sara said as she made her way to the door. At that moment the desk phone began to ring, Louise picked it up to answer and became aware that Sara was still lurking as her shadow gave away her presence. Annoyed Louise managed to reach the door with her foot and give it a firm kick shut.

'Yes Emily, I'm still here, just pushed the door shut, noisy in the corridors,' Louise said. 'Is Alan ok?'

'His family are with him but he's so unpredictable, vulnerable, good he's officially off, probably a month or so, depends.' Emily reported.

'I've had Sara snooping around here, she says she was Janie's friend and knew Alan too?'

'Oh I had no idea of that?' Emily sounded surprised.

*

It was a bright sunny day with not a cloud in sight. The air temperature was fresh and generally quite pleasant, if it hadn't been for the occasion, it could have been a great day.

Standing around trying to avoid eye contact with each of the bereaved was interminable, like waiting for an exam result. At least that would have ensured a celebration or better luck next time reaction but this was just waiting and knowing the worst of the pain is to come.

As more people arrived, so did a sense of anger at being cheated of a young woman who was so popular with so much to live for and who died because of a freak weather condition. There were no raised voices but the odd murmur, like a wave of trepidation and compassion. There was nothing to distract the inner sadness as the procession of people followed the minister into the crematorium to Michael Jackson's Earth Song that Janie had loved so much.

Emily and David sidled along a row of seats, closely followed by a steady stream of mourners and eventually the whole chapel was packed tight. Emily sadly took the opportunity to glance at the settling congregation. Aware that someone was looking at her she turned her head slightly further, straight into the face of Sara, who gave a wan smile. Emily quickly turned back, nudged David and whispered.

'Huh… a not-so-popular member of my team is here, highly inappropriate as far as I'm concerned.'

'You can't stop people from paying their respects, Em,' he whispered back as Jackson, now in full swing, sang out his earth song.

'Highly inappropriate, she hardly knew Alan.'

'Shush,' he said and turned his head to see who she was talking about then he stared straight in to the face of a sly smiling Sara. Jesus Christ what the hell is she doing here, he thought?

At the wake, groups huddled together, clearly feeling safe with their own conversations. It seemed that any outside contribution made for an uncomfortable interaction and to say too little, not wanting to engage too deeply, too near the mark or say something accidently could trigger a tearful response. It was like treading on eggshells.

Home-made cakes lay untouched, it seemed such a waste of good food. Slowly the wake members started to leave allowing the grieving family to their work. Alan moved around in a day dream, his best mate gone forever.

13

As she stood in the operating theatre her eyes darted back and forth and around, then up to where Owen was standing. He was now busy reversing the effects of anaesthesia on the patient lying on a trolley bed. Not once did he look over at her, she would have been aware if he had. Instead she had watched him throughout the whole procedure. She moved her surgical trolley aside so she could do a one last check of the sharps, all needles and blades correct and all swabs accounted for. Slowly and meticulously she went through the instrument check list with her runner, who kept trying to speed up this process, but Sara would not tolerate this. Instead she stopped her counting and stared at her runner, who shook and rustled the crumpled check list, as if to say, get on with it. Sara waited for a moment, as if to provoke the situation further then stated that she would not be hurried and that she was accountable for her trolley. The runner rolled her eyes in despair, took a deep breath and deliberately spoke slowly reading each syllable as if to a child. Sara went along with this pretence, knowing the runner would soon tire of this sarcasm. A voice broke her concentration.

'No lost needle then Sara?' Owen said with a smirk on his face.

'Should I have?' she said indignantly

'Well there's a lot lost recently, particularly when you're around, not just needles!'

Sara glanced around the theatre, everyone was busy going about their business not wanting any involvement, no one. She chose to ignore this comment and as Owen pushed past her, he held her gaze for just a moment, enough to give a contemptable sneer. She became hot wearing her surgical mask so pulled it down to breathe. The air was still pungent from the diathermy use and she hated taking in a deep breath. He then called over his shoulder as he disappeared in to the corridor that led to the recovery room. His voice carried along with him but loud enough for all to hear.

'Oh by the way, Laura, doesn't ask after you, well, only through a solicitor's letter,' he said sarcastically. 'Any comment?'

Sara slammed her trolley into the wall just as Louise appeared at the open theatre doors and on feeling the tension within the theatre she considered deploying Sara elsewhere. The unrest had grown since the death of Janie and somehow it was unclear how it could have escalated to this crisis. There must be more going on, thought Louise then she went in search of Emily.

*

Just for a moment David sat down with his cup of tea to do the crossword. But first he flitted through the obituaries as he always did then took a sip of the steaming hot liquid letting out a satisfied sigh when he was suddenly startled by the spare phone ringing. He had no intention of answering it and next time he saw Sara he'd give it back to her. The sooner the better, he wanted nothing more to do with her. What the fuck was she doing at the crematorium, he thought?

The doorbell rang, longer than was necessary, someone was determined to get attention. It irritated David, it was such an intrusion, bordering on rude. He nipped up to the front bedroom window that over looked the gravelled car park. A lone white car was neatly positioned, he didn't recognise it a first and so wondered if it was an Amazon delivery, for Emily. He quickly rounded the bed and made his way back down the stairs to open the front door, not expecting to find Sara standing there. She smiled at his shocked expression.

'Hello David thought I'd pop in and see how you are doing,' she said, 'I did phone you beforehand. Your special phone I gave you?'

'What?' he said, glancing at his watch and staring past her down his driveway.

'Aren't you going to ask me in, David?'

'I don't think so,' he barked, 'my wife will be home shortly and I would rather you go,' he said with a nervous gulp hoping she didn't notice.

'Oh don't worry about Emily, she's very busy and won't be back for some time, I do actually work with her you know?' She flicked her long hair back over her shoulder leaving a few strands that floated each time when caught on a breeze.

'You can take your bloody phone while you're here,' he turned and walked back up the hall and into his study where he kept it in his holdall. As he turned he almost fell over her, she had been right behind him. He was so angry that he thrust the phone into her hands.

'Here,' he said, 'now leave.' He gave an extenuated sweep with his arm as if swatting a fly.

'Thank you,' she said in a meek seductive tone.

'Oh and before you go why were you at the funeral?'

'Janie was my friend and of course Alan was too.'

'Alan was?'

'Yes I'm afraid so.' She gave a knowing smile as if to taunt.

'Had him on your phone list I suppose?'

'Maybe,' she wobbled her head and her dark green eyes grew more oriental than usual.

'Just get out!'

'Okay, I'll leave your stuff with Emily then?'

'Get out!' he shouted as he stumbled towards her.

'Oh by the way did you like your take-away the other week, thought I'd get you something after all I felt mildly responsible for your bad luck, you know, your kitchen fire?' She turned and walked out of his house got into her car, turned her head and gave a small wave as she drove off. David - now incensed almost choked on his own spittle.

Instantly he regretted his sudden outburst, he become overcome with fear and shame. He imagined Emily hearing of his past infidelity, all his lies. He needed to see Mark, confess his disloyalty at least that would be one shocked person out of the way. It would only be a matter of time before it became common knowledge anyway. He could feel sweat on his brow and as his stomach churned he grabbed his keys, went out to his car and on his way phoned Mark, to make sure he'd be at home.

'Hi Mark I've got a problem and wondered if I could run it by you,' David said aware of the crunching gravel under his feet.

'Ah good and I need to run one by you too. Are you back as a solicitor yet?' Mark asked.

'I'm working on it,' David said grumpily.

'You sound in a bad way my friend.'

'I am and you can't imagine what I've done to get there.'

'I'm intrigued,' Mark said, 'oh and according to Emily I was supposed to have left a spare mobile phone with you?'

David ignored Mark's comment and said. 'Look… I'll see you in ten minutes,' then hung up.

It started to rain, a fine drizzle a fine type that left the screen wipers smearing up a mess. David waited 'til it cleared with the help of the screen washer then sped off in a wheel spin, gravel flying all over the place. Some of it landed on the winter grass. His tyres left empty ruts that now lay open to the elements.

*

Sara stood outside waiting for her taxi, the same firm every time. It almost felt a relief that she had accomplished what she thought would allow her to move on with her life. A certain amount of euphoria rushed through her as the dazzling headlights pulled up next to her.

14

Initially he had felt fit for nothing after his discharge from the army. He so loved the action, getting all kitted out in camouflage whether he was in a wooded area or in the desert. It was the camaraderie he yearned for though, the mates he learned to trust. . . he missed the smell of a fry-up in the open air, the sizzling sound of fat splashing and popping out of the pan and the orderly queues of army personnel all concentrating on the food they were about to heap on to their plates. The very thought of this brought a smile to Daniel's face.

There was nothing more satisfying than seeing your face in the final shine on your boots and the whiff of the boot polish which stayed for a long while in the nostrils. He reminisced the sounds of boots marching in perfect sequence, the sergeant's orders and parade time salute to the commanding officer. Pride. Now at last, he could reflect back without fear and anger, just sadness, emptiness.

The cognitive treatment he got from the army's therapist, was sort of helpful once he got the hang of the technique, so called diversional therapy, even though he still felt shit. He would always remember his anger and fear in the early days which would render him in a permanent state of stress, uncontrollable shaking and palpitations which sounded more like drums in his ears. Even now on some days he found just that little thing, like a sound or a smell, would be a trigger to set him off. At least he had some control and knew the attacks would become less as time went by, he hoped.

Daniel wasn't sure what was expected of him, he now had this phone with bizarre numbers scribed on it, why three, four, six he thought? Sara said she'd phone him later she liked to dictate their liaisons and usually he like the distraction, she certainly knew how to entertain. But to phone at eight that evening was now inconvenient as he was hoping to meet Lizzie for a meal, a kind of date to rekindle their relationship. He felt a fool for getting sucked in to Sara's charms, it just added to his problems, a commitment he could do without. It made sense to book a table for eight thirty, this would give him ample time to get Sara's phone call out of the way.

The Red Lion was a nice pub, Daniel had been there a few times before and it was where he met up with Sara on their first date. Its reviews were glowing so without hesitation he booked a table for two at eight thirty. This would allow him time to deal with Sara's call. Perfect plan he thought. He sat back in his chair drinking a lager and contemplating this thought, he smiled to himself and shook his head. No way could he carry on, no way. It's got to finish.

There was a crowd of lads nearby in the open-plan bar who were in full swing, laughing and telling jokes. Daniel sat in the restaurant area with low lights that created a more intimate atmosphere just the sort of feel for his reunion. He looked down at his jeans and wondered if he had dressed too casually, perhaps he could've worn some chinos but then he didn't want to look overplayed for this occasion. He checked his breath in his cupped hand, ok, acceptable beer breath and wondered if he should've got some gum or something. He shrugged to himself as he felt an inner calm. He continued to gaze at the manic road users, waiting for Sara to phone - and then his true date.

Sara smiled smugly to herself, it was almost eight o'clock. She sat with a glass of chilled wine as she watched her kitchen clock tick away its seconds. She believed women had this irresistible effect on men, it certainly did on her father who spent much of his time with his lover. It made her angry just thinking of the destruction it had on her family, her dear mother. She took out her new perfume, Poison and sprayed some on each side of her neck, where some of it ran down slowly 'til it settled and dried, giving off its full scent. She thought back to the day in Emily's office where she first discovered this lovely perfume.

She became excited at the prospect of speaking to Daniel knowing he would be the last of her chosen men. She went over to her chiffonier pulled open its top drawer and touched the water colour painting of the rabbit. Daniel's, she said to herself. Then from her handbag she took out her phone and scrolled her address book to the numbers three four six and pressed call. He answered on the second ring.

'Hello,' he said at the same time as the crowd of young lads started to laugh.

'Hello Daniel sounds like you're having fun and without me,' she said.

'Oh it's just a few lads passing by,'

'Would you like dinner with me tonight?'

'Well not tonight, Sara,' he paused. 'I don't think this is going to work, you and me, sorry, but…'

'Ok, another time perhaps?' She would not show her disappointment because she didn't know how to. She often felt devoid of emotions but she did feel bothered enough as she was used to planning and smooth running.

'No, I'll be honest, I'm not sure what I want at the moment and this just complicates things.'

'Ok.' Then she hung up. She was unfazed by what he said. He'll change his mind when he thinks of all the fun they could have had, she thought. Then she checked the app on her phone to find Daniel's location, The Red Lion pub pulsed away. She gave herself a mischievous smile and said out loud to no one. 'Where we had our first date, how romantic. I wonder who he's meeting there tonight.' She sat pondering for a few moments then held her finger up as if she had an idea, got up from her seat and put her wine down on its mat. She went upstairs to her bedroom and found a heavy plastic bag neatly folded in her en-suite cabinet drawer and started to place items inside it.

The lads at the corner table were laughing and enjoying their evening. It brought back memories of Daniel's younger days and then to his lost mates…He hung his head in his hands and rubbed his face hard. Then he stood up and went over to the bar, appreciating the early booking of the table as more people arrived. He bought another pint of beer and made his way back over to his reserved table and sat down. He put his beer on the little cardboard mat advertising Dark Star Ales and looked around at his surroundings. There were only six tables in this part of the restaurant and each one had the same beer mats and in the centre of each table were baskets with cutlery wrapped in white paper napkins, waiting for use. Glass candle holders with lit candles flickered and wafted a fragrance each time the pub door opened which created an informal and cosy atmosphere for the diners so hopefully Lizzie would feel relaxed.

He sat opposite the window that looked out on to the entrance porch to where the taxis parked. He checked his watch, eight forty five. Lizzie was late.

He needed a pee so he nipped out to the toilet leaving his beer on the table when a taxi arrived but he wasn't there to see who got out and entered the pub. On his return he sat back in his seat with a more comfortable bladder and took a swig from his beer. As he looked up Sara was standing there, smiling. He almost dropped his glass.

'What the fuck...' he said, clearly not pleased to see her. 'Why are you here?'

'A surprise visit.' Sara said with a sour smile on her face.

She sat down in the empty chair opposite. 'Aren't you going to offer me drink?' she said.

'Not bloody likely... you're invading my space, just leave me alone!'

'Oh dear,' she said and started to rummage in her large Burberry tote bag, searching like an excited child in a wild kind of frantic quest. 'Ah here we are.' She plonked a heavy plastic carrier bag on the table and in doing so managed to flap the flimsy paper menu on to the floor but made no attempt to pick it up.

His throat started to constrict and he found it difficult to swallow, he could feel sweat forming on his brow and under his nose, he wiped it with the back of his hand as he started to shake uncontrollably. Then without thinking he swiped the bag off the table, knocking his glass of beer in its wake onto the floor, it exploded in to tiny pieces, alerting one of the bar staff. 'Hey what's your game mate...you'll have to pay for damages

Prior to her Death

you know.' But Daniel didn't hear him or anyone else as he disappeared back to the time in Afghanistan and all that noise.

The lads on the other side of the bar could hear the commotion and knew there was trouble and rushed round in case a fight broke out. They saw Sara surrounded by broken glass. They became concerned for her safety.

'Come on mate, calm yourself down, you're frightening the lady,' one of the bigger lads said. Daniel stayed seated on his chair, his head in his hands as he rocked intensely back and forth. The bar man confirmed that the police were now on their way. One of the lads tried to have a conversation with Daniel with no response then looked up at Sara, who stood by indifferently still holding her large hand bag. It didn't take the police long to arrive, and one officer tactfully approached Daniel. 'What's going on sir?' It was clear that Daniel was not going to communicate with anyone, so the officer tried again, 'I think we'd better get you home and calmed down sir,' and started to help him to stand. Then the bar man called out to the police officer.

'He'd booked that table for the two of them, probably a row,' said the bar man who pointed to Sara. Another police officer followed his gaze to Sara, who stood quietly clutching her bag. Her face didn't give anything away as she kept looking at the pub door as if in a world of her own. Both the officers looked at each other with puzzled frowns.

'Are you with this man?' asked the officer.

'No not me, he's waiting for his dinner guest apparently,' Sara said coldly.

As if on cue Lizzie walked into the pub, she stopped when she saw Daniel with the police officer.

'What's going on here?' Lizzie asked no one in particular. She met Sara's eyes as she turned to Sara and asked. 'Do you know what's going on?'

Sara acted as if pleased to see Lizzie and moved towards her talking as if nothing had happened, as if they were old chums.

'Ah here you are, you must be his dinner guest?' Said Sara in an expectant tone.

'Yes… what's been happening? Lizzie asked Sara.

'It's this bag of toiletries that belongs to Danny, he left them in my bathroom. I don't want them cluttering up the place, now that he's left.'

'Left, left what. . ?' Lizzie was bewildered as she watched helplessly whilst Daniel was taken out of the pub, he hadn't noticed Lizzie, even when she called his name.

'Oh God he's lost it again.' She half mumbled but the bar man heard her.

'Well if he can't hold his alcohol he shouldn't drink it,' he said, 'he threw the table over and frightened his lady friend.'

'What lady friend?'

'Her behind you…he'd booked that table for the two of them.' A bewildered Lizzie spun round to the toiletry bag woman who now stood with downcast eyes and when she looked up at Lizzie there was mock shame in them.

'Ah my taxi.' Sara whispered to herself as she checked her watch and left the pub, in a rush, like the white rabbit in Alice in Wonderland.

15

The slam of a door echoed somewhere within the theatre suite, silence followed for a few minutes then the sound of running footsteps…fading off into the distance. A swish from a self-closing fire door which then bumped shut. Moments later the whoosh of a separate door opening in another direction just beyond the passage that surrounded the theatre known as the dirty corridor.

The cacophony from the metal covers on the laminar air flow system flapped frantically in an uncoordinated and confused state. It was the interrupted air that changed their pressure. The natural course of forcing contaminated air out whilst bringing in the fresh had always been part of the infection control system. The metal covers mapped the flow of extra pressure on opening and closing doors.

A sudden blast of heavy breathing like that of a banshee sighing propelled its sinister groan around what seemed like the inside of a small compartment. Short sharp bouts of forced air through a narrow tube, similar to that of a tyre pump, the type in a garage that spits out its pressure in controlled bursts. Then silence… only broken by something, like a piece of light plastic of some sort, which hit the floor's surface and rolled with little resistance until it stopped abruptly against something hard. Footsteps, urgent, quick and determined moved in to another room after another swish of a door in motion and then tearing of paper- packets could be heard, clearly at first, then as the door started to close, faded to a bump.

A barely audible voice quietly cursed as it appeared harried and incoherent. The jangling keys were clearly, actively opening a lock and for a split second it appeared the muted operator could be heard contemplating, selecting items. The sound of purposeful movement from one room to another livened the laminar air flow in to a crescendo that drowned out, whatever other goings on within.

A strange muffled human type cry came from under what seemed like a sealed entity, a breathing apparatus of some kind that wheezed and whistled, sucking in and out, gassiness. Something hard and heavy fell to the floor like a brick and pieces could be heard flying from it like beads across the tiles as it shattered.

*

At seven o'clock the lift door opened and out got Jim Crosby pushing his well-stocked housekeeping trolley in to the main corridor. He looked at his night time reflection in the windows as he manoeuvred along the way, admiring his new haircut and trimmed cavalier type beard, both still dark brown. He was in no hurry, although he should have been as usually there were two for this job. His shift finished at ten tonight and he was in no mood to stay any later than that. In fact the earlier he could finish, the better. He strolled into the reception area and parked his trolley, just to make it look authentic, he unloaded the paper towels from its top and piled them high on the desk. He then slid the mops out of the purpose built holders at the front and placed them precariously against a wall where one mop managed to topple over on to its side. He added some containers of cleaning stuff then surveyed his display with a smile before making his way to the staff room.

Rubbing his dry hands together his first thought was a coffee and some of the homemade cake that is always topped up on a daily basis by the dedicated bakers amongst the staff. Some of the cakes were gluten free and in a separate box, so he didn't bother with them. He sat down in an arm chair, clasping his hot drink in one hand and checking the cake container in the other. As it was clear plastic he could see at a glance what was in store for him tonight, fruit cake and Victoria sponge, so he took a piece of each then picked up the Shoreham Herald. As he flitted through he spotted an article that was about Janie Clarke, the wife of a theatre manager, who had died tragically in a flood a couple of weeks ago. Old news he thought then turned the page over to auto sales.

It was the sudden noise that startled him, he looked up, it was different somehow and he wasn't quite sure in which way. He glanced up at the wall clock that hung on a stark white background, it showed almost seven thirty which Jim knew was always a few minutes slow. He immediately thought of his kids and hoped that they would have an early night ready for their holiday tomorrow. Erring on the side of caution, he stood up and looked out of the staff room door anyway. The sound didn't seem to come from around the reception area, even so just in case his boss had sneaked up on a spot check, he went out and plugged his vacuum cleaner in to the socket then took a pack of paper hand towels back to the staff room. He finished his coffee and scoffed the remainder of his cake when he thought he saw a shadow, peripherally, through the obscure type glass within the outside passage known as the dirty corridor that passed around the theatres and alongside the staff room.

'Hello?' he said and waited for a reply. He felt he wasn't alone but no one would be here now all the staff would have left at least an hour ago. He checked his watch, seven fifty pm and wondered if one of them had been carrying out some kind of audit. Often he'd find a thick theatre log book left on the secretary's desk when they should have been locked in the store cupboard, under Archived. He felt goose bumps.

The sudden commotion from the laminar covers startled Jim further, maybe he should phone his supervisor for reassurance, but then he thought maybe not, as he still hadn't quite started his cleaning. He had his little routine and didn't want to be sussed out, no he didn't want that to happen.

His mind raced back to the unfamiliar sound in the staff room earlier, not usual for that time of night and thought he'd recognised what caused the noise. It had only ever happened before when pressure from the open doors led out to the clean and dirty corridors and would close simultaneously. It causes the covers to flap, yeah, that was it and someone had used the dirty corridor at the time when he was in the staff room. He felt quite proud of his scientific deduction.

It was the abrupt swish of a door closing, from within one of the staff changing rooms, that activated movement in the air flow system and Jim almost ran back into the staff lounge hoping to catch a glimpse of someone leaving but the shadow moved too quickly. Jim knew he would never catch up with whoever it was. The shadow's quickened footsteps could be heard as they disappeared into the distance, down the stairs into the main hospital leaving in its wake the fire exit door from the dirty corridor to click shut. Because Jim was too late and annoyed he shouted after to whoever it was leaving.

'Excuse me, but its late you know, it would have been nice to have known you were here!' Then under his breath he added, 'Arsehole.'

It had taken Jim on his own, a good hour just emptying and loading each contaminated refuse sack into the huge metal cages and washing the floor as he went. He busied himself with making up the cleaning solution for the laborious washing down of dirty theatre furniture and equipment that often had blood and gore stubbornly stuck to them. It made him shudder with disgust at the thought and it was just as well that most of the equipment and furniture had been stacked outside the open doors to each theatre. This allowed him to mop the floors with the strong chemical solution allowing quick drying time. His route of cleaning never deviated as he would start in the changing rooms, this included theatre shoes of various kinds, bags of used uniforms, some of which hung haplessly over the side of its sack, waiting for him to put them in properly. There was always this smell of sweat and cheese that reminded Jim of his own sports bag, before and after his football matches, it infiltrated everything, even lingered in his nose.

He felt increasingly uneasy about something he'd missed. He sat down on an old wooden bench that lined one wall of the room and began wiping the shoes. He yawned noisily as no one was around to hear him which made him chuckle out loud. This was his last shift before his holiday with his wife and children and he wondered how the kids would cope with the long flight to Florida, a promise he made them all last year. With a bit of luck he'd get off early tonight and he had already decided to leave some of the cleaning like the staff room and kitchen. Rach would be pleased with his help with the last of the suitcase packing and weighing them to make sure they met the airline's rules.

Still deep in thought and in a reflective mood, he began to analyse the previous sounds and late staff, when an unexpected alarm sounded in the clean corridor. It quickly shook him out of his trance, he jumped up and at almost a run, rushed to where the source of the noise came from. Ahead of him was a panel showing a flashing light, indicating that one of the anaesthetic gases was at low pressure, he thought it strange and took a photo of it on his phone just in case it suddenly stopped as he'd never remember which light was flashing. He then alerted Viv, his supervisor.

Puzzled by the night's events so far, he looked around and listened not sure if he had heard a door swish or perhaps it was the fridge cooling sound or maybe his supervisor arriving? Laminar air flow covers flapped as pressure changed within the theatre, now he wondered if the low pressure of the gas had caused it all along, and he suddenly felt foolish. Then he heard one of the cages being pushed hard up against the wall and quick footsteps disappearing off in to the distance, the open swish of a fire door, then its click shut. Jim shook his head and called out.

'Hello!'

No answer.

He looked around at where he had cleaned earlier, only one more theatre to do now. He could feel the hairs on the back of his neck stand up, he was frightened he didn't mind admitting it. Thank God not long till he'd be out of there tonight he thought. He left his trolley outside the scrub area and with a plastic bucket he entered it to give the large trough type sinks a good wipe down and then when finished he left to clean the furniture from outside of the theatre. There was a cool draft coming from somewhere and he followed it to a half open fire door that led out into the dirty corridor, it had been deliberately left ajar, he went over to inspect it and found a rolled up draw sheet placed as a wedge.

There had been a recent spate of thefts from hospitals around the county and now Jim suspected that all the night's activity was actually theft in progress. He felt daft he'd not spotted the tell-tale signs earlier. Then he noticed that one of the operating tables was not outside, waiting for its usual clean, shit it's been stolen he thought. He hadn't noticed that the double theatre doors were still closed too.

The intermittent acoustics of the metal flaps were still too active in the theatre. It could be because the door to the dirty corridor had been left open. Jim stood deliberating as he gazed at the closed theatre double doors. Why were they still closed…possibly someone had forgotten to leave them open and maybe just maybe the operating table was still inside? The alarm hummed happily and he found he hardly noticed it at all now. He continued to wipe down what was left and as he worked his way towards the doors he could see that he'd have to move some stuff away before he could open them. He dragged the wheelie chairs out first then a large trolley that had been overstocked with items and as he moved it forward some of the items fell to the floor. Jim cursed.

The smell of old perished rubber much like an old hot water bottle, wafted from another trolley that had been laden with arm supports and small pressure pads. As he pulled them apart, their surfaces which had stuck together, made a tearing scrunch sound. At last he reached one of the doors and partially pulled it open with his foot pressed down on the bottom door stop to anchor it.

A distant phone started to ring, as far away as in the reception area, but Jim chose to ignore it after all he'd almost finished his cleaning and no way was he going to do any extra overtime, especially tonight. He looked up at the clock on the wall, twenty one thirty hours then stopped…. his eyes darted about, disbelieving what was in front of him, his mouth open. The sudden rush of adrenaline made his heart beat fast and erratically in his ears, he felt nauseous. His fear grew.

It was quiet in this theatre, no air flow flap sounds, maybe because he'd left the door open? He wasn't quite sure what he was listening out for but he listened as he studied the scene before him not sure what to think or what to do, only that the place had driven him mad all evening and now this…

The recumbent person lying on the operating table remained very still…asleep Jim wondered? He inched his way forward slowly, not sure if he should disturb this person, possibly a woman… long strands of hair confirmed it was a woman. It was hard to see her breathing as she had her back to him, but then he thought that maybe she had just taken a nap, although rather bizarre on such a narrow mattress under intense lighting.

'Hello,' he whispered not wanting to startle her. No answer. He moved closer and tentatively around to face her properly. Her mouth was partially open in a natural pose of sleep, but there was dried fatty and slightly shiny residue of a substance that routed a straight line over her face as if something had been spilled, as if someone had reached over her, that was Jim's first thought.

She reminded him of a porcelain doll, petit with black, long hair that was partially held in a cap. He felt uncomfortable with the situation and spoke straight to her face, waiting for her to flinch her eyes open.

'Are you okay?' he said feeling spooked and as there was no response, deep down he knew she was dead.

There was something on the floor just under the operating table castor that caught his eye, a smart phone? It had a cracked and smashed screen and as he picked it up he could see immediately that the compartment where the sim card should have been yielded an empty space. A piece of its plastic glass pinged to the hard floor so he automatically stooped to pick it up and noticed more small shards, presumably from the screen. He carefully picked up the pieces and chucked them into a nearby sharps box, the rest of the phone he put into his bag as he thought it may be useful with a new sim, battery and front that he'd get from Amazon or Ebay later.

A strange notion went through his mind. If he had made a William Hill bet, a million to one chance, to have found someone dead in this environment, it could've turned him into an overnight millionaire, he smiled to himself, then shamefully he wondered if this was his way of coping, a form of hysteria. He quickly went over to the hospital phone in the corner of the theatre he must let Viv know what has happened. It answered on the third ring, it was Viv.'

'Hello housekeeping supervisor,' the detached voice said calmly.

'Viv, there's a dead woman in theatre four, what shall I do…. it's awful…the whole evening's been a nightmare,' Jim said in the weary tone of an exasperated man. Then he found himself in a yawn, straight down into the phone and wondered what his boss thought of this unguarded action, after all he was tired out with all the evening interruptions…

'There's someone dead in the theatre?' she echoed back to Jim in an incredulous tone.

'Yes, she looks dead and doesn't answer when I call her…' It went quiet on the other end of the phone for just a few seconds, before Viv responded.

'Don't touch anything, make your way to the reception and I'll meet you there.'

16

Harry watched his wife, Julie, folding the sheets in an almost expert way. They rarely ironed any of them because according to her, she reckoned if you remove them from the tumble dryer whilst still hot, they would not crease. Fair enough thought Harry.

Harry loved his small hotel of eight en-suite bedrooms and had always wanted to be a Company Director and now here he was, just that. Julie often scolded him for being big headed especially when he answered the phone announcing, 'Knutsford House, proprietor speaking' or in his emails he'd put Company Director. It was the best thing he'd ever done apart from marrying, this often elusive Detective Inspector with the Shoreham Police. He never minded her job, he was proud of her but sometimes he worried when it involved criminal gangs, knives and shotguns. She did take care not to put herself in the line of fire wearing a Kevlar vest but still he worried. Being part of the Major Crime Team or otherwise known as MCT, another section of the CID meant completing a usual shift, nine to five, but still remaining on call twenty-four-seven.

Tonight the last day of November he watched her as she busied herself with the laundry, her serious expression as she emptied the tumble drier, brought a smile to his face, imagining what her colleagues would think of her brief domesticity.

Even though her shift had finished at five she was still technically on call with the MCT and as it was technically Friday, the beginning of the weekend, she knew anything could happen. She was tempted to open a bottle of Merlot but she resisted, not good to smell of alcohol if she's called out. Instead she continued to smooth out the sheets, fold them and carriy them upstairs to the special linen cupboard on the first floor landing. The aroma of clean sheets made her linger a little longer than necessary just as a couple of guests passed her. She pretended to be sorting through the pillow cases and gave a brief acknowledgement with a smile and a nod.

In the distance a mobile phone started ringing, she recognised her ring tone, Twist and Shout by the Beatles, she quickly locked the cupboard door and dashed off to answer it. She had this dreadful thought as to whether she'd brought home her office phone as she had a strong feeling that she'd left it on her desk…shit no…it was still at work, she remembered now…this was a disciplinary. Feeling hot and bothered she ran down the stairs in a panic, past the earlier couple, apologising to them for startling them and when she reached the bottom step, met Harry who had just come out of the kitchen carefully carrying a tray of condiments. She heard them slide and chink together as he stopped abruptly and giving him an apologetic look, she grabbed her personal mobile, two missed calls from Shoreham Police station and one from the new Detective constable, Steve Hayes. She phoned him back immediately as Harry and the two guests stood by watching her.

'Ma'am, you left your phone here so I had to phone your own mobile,' he said.

'What is it?' Julie asked overlooking that fact.

'A suspicious death at Southlands Hospital, Old Shoreham Road in Shoreham,' said her new DC Steve Hayes.

'I know where Southlands Hospital is Steve,' she said irritated, 'SOCO there?'

'Yes and uniform. They've secured it as a crime scene.'

'I should bloody well hope so,' she said rolling her eyes as she shook her head. She would never do that in front of her Detective Constable as he had only recently joined the department and didn't want to knock his confidence. She made a mental note to thank him for contacting her personal mobile.

'I'll pick you up on my way, ma'am, say five minutes?'

'Yep, five minutes and bring my phone with you,' she hung up and let out a big sigh.

Harry, still holding the tray, gave a wan smile, 'Okay, I heard the conversation, see you at... some time then?' he said.

'Oh Harry, I left my work phone on my office desk!' She exclaimed.

The two guests stood in the hall watching the panic, 'Do you need a lift anywhere?' one of them asked as Harry turned to them and reassured them.

'No, no she has a lift about to arrive, thanks all the same,' He said, then in a whisper, 'she's a Detective Inspector in the CID, police, emergency...,' he aimed a nod at the front door as Julie opened it to Steve, 'that's her lift.'

Even before she had clicked her seat belt Steve was already out on the road with blues and twos in motion.

'What have we got?' Julie asked.

'A female wearing theatre scrubs found dead on an operating table in one the theatres, cause of death not sure. No sign of a struggle. Nurse Manager will meet us at the hospital entrance. Uniform have questioned the night housekeeper who found the body.' Steve reeled off.

'No operations on the go?'

'No. They finished at six pm.'

'What about emergencies?'

'No they do elective operations.'

They arrived in the hospital car park, which appeared more like a demolition site due to the ongoing building alterations and additions. The whole hospital had changed shape recently and now resembled more of a walk-in clinic.

At the entrance, as planned, the theatre nurse manager was waiting for them, clearly anxious as she was moving from one foot to the other, she probably had a glass of wine waiting for her at home thought Julie. Also she probably doesn't work weekend shifts due to elective surgery.' 'I'm Emily Lewis, theatre manager,' she said, about to proffer her hand but thought differently and stopped. 'The deceased is, was, a staff nurse here, her name is Sara Eaton, I have her address for you,' she passed a piece of paper to Julie. 'She lives alone as far as I know. I'm not sure on her private life but I'll check in the personal files in my office and let you know.'

'Okay, well I'm Detective Inspector Robertson and this is Detective Constable Hayes,' Julie pointed for the manager to go inside then followed her up to the first floor to where the theatres were, 'how many people were on duty this evening from six o'clock?'

'Oh... well the housekeepers, that is the supervisor, who assesses the area to see if two night housekeepers would be needed, then there is the delivery of surgical drapes, collection of cages and CSSD who take and bring instruments.' The manager puffed out her cheeks then sighed deeply. She appeared very nervous and she had an irritating habit of blowing rogue hair strands from her face as if she had some form of Tourette's syndrome.

'Do you have CCTV in operation?' Julie asked.

'Well...we do have them installed but I doubt very much they are working, although maybe in the outpatient department...' the manager said unsure.

Julie could hear doors opening and swooshing shut along the dark corridors then a breeze of uncertain cold stale air drifted in its wake, it made her shudder as she imagined the mortuary was somewhere along the way. She'd been to a few post mortems during her career but still she dreaded it when she had to visit the place. The smell of it.

'Hayes, put a check on the night housekeeper and get a quick statement from him,' Julie said, 'also has the rest of the team arrived yet?'

'Yes ma'am the team have just taken the theatre register, deceased's handbag and a computer for analysis from the crime scene.'

The usual plastic over shoes, overalls and gloves were immediately issued to Julie and Steve as they arrived at the crime scene. An unfamiliar acrid smell wafted through the air as if someone had dropped a bottle of some sort of chemical. She shuddered at that thought as she stood taking in the scene before her and studying the exits and fire doors with in the theatre. The clanging of the metal flaps intrigued her and she crouched to study one of them. DC Mark James, an experienced detective, told her what their purpose was and how they worked, Julie seemed satisfied with that. Then she said, 'Had the house keeper noticed any increased noise from these flaps?'

'Steve has just let him go home, ma'am,' said DC James.

'Oh never mind, we'll get a full statement from him tomorrow.'

When the forensic pathologist had moved back from the body, Julie surveyed what laid before her from head to foot making mental notes. The Pathologist Adam Cotter looked up at Julie and said. 'Oriental, petit about four foot ten inches, near her tiny left hand an empty syringe was found, long straight black hair, no jewellery as such, bearing in mind that staff are not allowed to wear any, because of infection risk, so she had probably been on duty that day. In fact Sara Eaton looks like a little china doll,' he paused then went on, 'no immediate defence marks and there's a mark indicating cannula insertion on her left hand, some shiny and dried oily type substance around that site, possibly an anaesthetic agent of some kind. I've taken a swab from this for analysis also a syringe with some white substance was found nearby, possibly Propofol, looks like some bruising around the nose and mouth consistent with an anaesthetic mask being held tight and finger imprints under her jaw, all typical of anaesthetising. ETD probably within the last two hours which means between seven pm to nine pm at a guess.'

'Okay thanks Adam, we'll see you tomorrow? ' She looked up at Steve who nodded his agreement.

'I'll start early tomorrow, so don't worry too much about attending as there'll be plenty of photos.' Said Adam. 'By the way, face bruising is nearly post mortem, you know…'

The two path technicians, along with their opened mortuary bag, started to remove the body and as they did with little effort, a piece of paper fluttered down on to the floor from under the body's legs. Steve bent forward and quickly retrieved it, opened it up and read the simple typed text which said, 'I had endured enough and thought this to be my only way out and just wished that I had been a better person for you,' it was unsigned.

'Suicide?' said Steve.

'Strange note for a suicide and there's the finger imprints under her chin, a mystery,' said

Julie deep in thought, and then she said aloud, 'I'd better phone DCI Defoe, keep him sweet and up to speed.'

The theatre manager met Julie and Steve in the clean corridor just outside the theatre and gave them a list of staff who worked in the department or delivered or visited.

'Have you informed the next of kin?' asked Julie

'Yes, that would be her aunt in Kent, here's her address and contact number. She seemed to take it well and said she'd not seen Sara for the last year, only the occasional text or brief phone call.'

'We'll arrange for the family liaison officers to attend her,' said Julie.

'That's very thoughtful. I don't suppose her ex-husband should be informed too?'

Julie looked up with interest and glanced over at Steve who already had turned the page of his note book with pencil poised.

'Um, yes, please, thank you and we'd like his details too,' said Julie, 'had they been divorced very long?'

'Um only quite recently…think it was amicable…I didn't have much to do with her…my husband is friends with her ex,' the manager wrung her hands nervously, 'you know, rugby at school and such like, not my type either of them.'

'Either of them?' said Julie.

'No, well, the ex and…Sara.' she said mildly irritated and then she was distracted by the body bag being carried out, the shape of its deceased had obviously upset the manager as she brought her hand up to her mouth. Julie pressed on with another query.

'Oh, and one more thing, was Sara right or left handed?' asked Julie. The manager looked surprised and was clearly trying to remember.

'She was… left handed, yes definitely left handed.' she said emphatically.

Steve looked across to Julie, who nodded an acknowledgement to the manager.

'Does Sara Eaton have a locker here, any clothes in the changing room?' Julie queried.

'Yes I'll nip in and get them for you, one of your team has already taken the handbag.' said the manager and turned to go but was intercepted by Steve.

'No we'll get them as they are evidence, part of the crime scene, nothing must be touched, only by SOCO,' Steve said annoyed that the clothes had been overlooked.

'SOCO?' The manager queried.

'Yes Scenes of Crime Officers,' Steve added.

The laminar air flow covers continued their unusual noisy journey because now it was the toing and froing of police personnel who encouraged the covers to work overtime. Jim was relieved when he was allowed to go home - eleven thirty if you please. Tomorrow he and his family were off to Florida, Disney World, and nothing was going to mess this trip up. If Jim had told the detective about the holiday, it may well have been cancelled or he would not be allowed to go and Rach would not be a happy bunny, he thought. Jim's stomach churned just thinking of the dead woman and all the strange goings-on on his shift.

Anyway it didn't matter now that the deed was done and no way was Jim going to add any extra information at this time. He could always say later that he was anxious and tired and forgot about those strange things going on, yeah he thought convincing himself. He justified his actions by being in need of a holiday, you can't think straight when you're tired and shocked, he thought.

17

Emily barely remembered her drive back home because she was so preoccupied with Sara's strange death. It was near to one a. m. and she wondered whether she should have told David earlier but then she wasn't sure of the outcome. The note she left him just said, "Problem at the hospital, may be late." Knowing him he'd gone to bed.

She had been speeding along through the country lanes, haphazardly negotiating rain filled pot holes, each time she hit one it splashed muddy water up on to the already greasy window screen. She had the wipers on intermittent because it wasn't actually raining but it was enough for her it created smears, probably contaminated by farm manure and not helped by a virtually empty screen-wash bottle.

As she neared the turn off up her drive she could see that David was still up and no doubt waiting for her return. Now she would have to go through the whole ordeal again and he'll interrogate her like the solicitor he is or was.

Prior to her Death

As she got out of her car, David came out of the house to meet her.

'I know what's happened, Mark phoned briefly, no details as such,' David said excitedly.

'Good,' she said with a yawn.

'Sounds like she got what she deserved,' he said as he followed Emily in to the house.

'What?'

'A woman like that,' he shook his head slowly then said, 'bit off more than she could chew,'

'You said you didn't really know her, only seen her at Mark's, before their divorce?'

'Well I'm only saying what Mark had said.'

'You of all people, making that assumption without evidence.'

'I was his divorce solicitor you know and he told me she was psychopathic at times.'

'Well she bit off more than she could chew…and ended up dead.'

*

It was raining hard. Looking over the field at the river made Emily shiver. She was pleased it was Saturday, it meant she could have a lie in. She could hear David busy downstairs in the kitchen, his favourite place to be. She sat up and stretched, listening to rattling, possibly something on a tray? She suddenly felt special - he'd reach the top of the upstairs. Her anticipation was rewarded when he walked into the bedroom with a huge tray full of a variety of breakfast foods, most of which were cooked to perfection. He placed the tray on the chest near the window and Emily could see he'd prepared for two.

'Once you've eaten and taken a shower we could go out somewhere, it'll cheer you up,' he said.

'Well you do sound chirpy this morning David Lewis,' she said as she balanced a plate holding a boiled egg on her lap.

'I feel like a new man, it must be that diet I'm on, finally working.'

She looked up at him and yes he had lost that troubled look he'd been carrying around for the last few weeks. Not sure about his weight though, especially when he goes to try on his ski suit, she thought. She scooped out some runny egg yolk and relished its taste then dunked her fresh wholemeal soldier to soak up the rest...um delicious she thought.

A lone car turned in to their drive and slowly made its way to where Emily parked her car. The driver's door opened slowly and closed quietly. Mark got out and stood as if admiring the view, then he walked unhurriedly up to the front door, where it was opened by David. Mark looked glum and motioned to enter, David stood aside to let him in.

'I expect you've heard the details from Emily, Sara is no more,' he said as he plonked himself down on the sofa, 'I would say it looks suspicious David.'

'Yes it's a sorry day,' David shifted from one foot to the other.

'David, that phone you gave me wasn't mine, why did you give it to me?'

'It's a mystery phone from somewhere...,' David looked out the window as the sun came out from behind a mass of black clouds, 'um that's all I can say Mark.'

'Well did you notice the inscribed word ox and the strange numbers one and four or perhaps fourteen on the front? Looks like Sara's sort of handy work, sort of Chinese numbers of some kind. She was artistic as well as psychotic, probably goes hand in hand,' he rested his head back on a large Ikea cushion and remained in that position for a moment then brought his head back up and looked at David who appeared uncomfortable under Mark's stare.

'You said you met her privately about three weeks ago and she had flirted with you?'

'Yes just a quick meet in the high street,' he said dismissively, 'to tie up a few loose ends from your divorce or rather hers.'

Emily came down the stairs in her dressing gown, she recognised Mark's voice from the living room and went in to see him.

'Mark,' she said as she made her way over to him and bent down to give him a peck on the cheek, 'I'm sorry… the news and the whole business, I don't know what to say, as I know you and Sara were officially divorced…but still it must be a shock.'

'A shock yes and at the same time sad her life ended this way,' he said, 'I'm no psychologist but she needed help of some sort that was for sure.' Mark got up from the sofa and gave Emily a peck on the cheek before he turned to David. 'See me out David ol' boy,' he said with a smile. 'Goodbye Em, thanks for your kind words. Rotten job for you last night eh?' She nodded a reply not wanting to get involved with any details. DI Robertson had said she must not talk to anyone about the incident.

David was pleased that Mark was leaving, he felt uncomfortable as to what his purpose for being here was apart from needing to talk to someone? They made their way to the front door when Mark rounded on David.

'Were you having an affair with her?' Mark asked in almost a whisper.

'What…no way Mark. Strange thing to ask…' David's mouth went dry, he was conscious of licking his lips and hoped Mark had not noticed his anxiety. Instead David managed to laugh it off, nervously. Mark got in to his car and without looking up drove off.

He could hear Emily back upstairs moving around probably making the bed, then he heard the china rattling on the tray, tha e'd taken up to her earlier. It could have been a good start to a perfect today if Mark hadn't called round, snooping. After all it was a couple of weeks ago since he'd finished the affair. David heard Emily loading the dish washer, she was always careful how she stacked each item for best results, the door bounced shut and the cycle started. Fancy not remembering the numbers were on the front of that bloody phone, he thought now angry.

18

There were no sounds coming from the house. The blinds were half open as if the sun was glaring in on one of the occupants and dazzling them yet for them to be at that angle even the upstairs ones didn't make sense to detective constable Steve Hayes. He studied the door and its surrounds for a means of attracting attention, there was no knocker or bell in sight which left him no alternative but to bare knuckle rap. No answer, he tried again, waited a reasonable length of time then he tried the mobile number he was given hoping that someone would answer. In the distance somewhere inside the house he could hear a phone ringing, there was no voice mail so he tried it again and noticed at the same time he could hear the same ringing. He thought that someone had forgotten to take it with them. He rapped once more, taking in the front of the house which seemed well cared for and the garden looked neat for late November.

He wandered around to the side of the house and noticed a tall gate, about the same height as himself six two, so he could actually get a good look into the back garden, albeit on his toes. Then he tried the gate and sensibly found it was locked, he called out in case someone was nearby then he rattled the gate latch, no one answered him so he shouted a little louder. It started to rain and a gust of wind got up and blew in his ear, he pulled up his collar but it didn't protect him from the sudden downpour that trickled its way down the back of his neck, making him shiver.

Steve Hayes liked his new role in the CID and wanted to impress his DI. Although she was okay to work with, she could be very single minded too. At the morning briefing she gave out instruction commonly known as actions in the force. Because he'd already questioned Jim Crosby last night it was his follow up action today.

Suddenly a voice spoke, he turned to face a woman in a dressing gown. She didn't look too happy with him. 'Yes?' She said.

'Oh good morning, yes I need to see your neighbour and it seems he's not in at the moment, so I'll call back later,' Steve said with a smile, 'sorry to have disturbed you.'

'Shouldn't bother, he won't be in,' the woman said sternly.

'Oh well, do you know when he's likely to be in?'

'Who wants to know?'

Steve took out his police ID and flashed it at the woman. She took it from him and studied it then returned it with a friendlier attitude.

'Oh dear, hope there hasn't been a tragedy?' She said.

Steve didn't answer the question but followed it through with the usual course of enquiry.

'Do you know where I can contact Mr Crosby?' he asked.

'Well, not exactly, they all left about five a.m. this morning in a taxi,' she paused in thought, 'Disney World with the family, the Florida one, you know?'

Steve's heart leapt a beat, as he couldn't remember if he told Jim Crosby that he'd be back to see him and not to leave the country as it's a suspicious death, oh shit, he thought.

'How long have they gone for?'

'Oh they'll be back this time next week. Those kids were so looking forward to this trip, in fact all of them were,' she said wrapping her dressing gown around herself tightly just as another gust of wind howled its way into a pile of dead leaves that dispersed back around the garden, 'hard working family that.'

Steve let out a loud sigh. It was too wet to write all this in his note book and now he'd have to report back to his boss who was not going to be happy with this development, the main witness and possible suspect had left the country.

*

When the message and bleep confirmed it was safe to unfasten the seat belts, both the Crosby children wanted to walk up the aisles. Rachael Crosby put her husband in charge of them at this moment even though he was still jaded from last night's events and the early morning rise. All Jim wanted to do was catch up on his sleep but it was for his children that this holiday of a life time had happened. He did wonder if he should have mentioned this to the nice DC last night, but no point in ruining their holiday complicating things. He took the children to the toilet then back to their seats where they took turns to sit by the window. Rachael got out her phone and decided to change the time to Florida time. She looked at Jim, his eyes were closed and she quietly said, 'Jim are you going to change your phone time now, ready?'

'Okay,' then he put his hand into his back pocket as if to retrieve it but he had deliberately left it at home on the living room table, just in case the police wanted to contact him. 'Oh dear I think I've left it at home.' He looked over at her angry face.

'Jim how could you forget that?'

'I'll get a pay as you go job when we're out there, don't worry so,' he leant his head back deep in thought. 'Had a bad night at work, glad to be out of it.'

'What do you mean?'

'You might find this hard to believe but…' his eyes welled up.

'You've got the sack?'

'No, I found a dead woman in the theatre.' He let out a sigh of relief.

'Oh my God…why didn't you tell me…how awful for you…did you know her?'

'Nope, but she must have been one of the staff as she was still in theatre uniform.'

'What's going to happen now that you have left the country…that's called something, um,' she thought for a moment, 'I don't know…perverting the course of justice or something like that?' She paused in thought then said. 'They may think you killed her.'

'For God's sake Rach, you know that's not the case!' He swallowed hard and said. 'At least they can't get hold of me now I'm on holiday.'

'Don't you be too sure, if they know where you've gone they can check your details with the airline and you may find police waiting for you at the other end...American police or FBI and then we'll all be deported back as criminals.'

'Jesus Christ Rach, we're not terrorists!'

19

Each action given out by DI Julie Robertson during the morning meeting was received by a sleepy team; some looked bleary eyed, and some always appeared permanently tired and their yawing was not only infectious but distracting too. How it annoyed her, because whenever it was her rota, on duty with the major crime team, she'd keep off the booze and avoid dinners out, simple. But generally they all worked well together during the week when they were on MCT duty.

The display board on the office wall was already forming details with the deceased's photo and a few names of significant others, like the ex-husband, an aunt, the night housekeeper, his supervisor and the theatre manager all of which had connections to the deceased one way or another and then the strange note indicating suicide, at least it was a start. Julie wasn't convinced it was that, there was something about it that didn't make sense. Harry always said she had a suspicious mind, she smiled at that thought then she looked at her watch, four thirty and wondered if she'd make dinner on time later.

She was sitting in her swivel chair twisting side to side reading Jim Crosby's statement of events and every so often she picked up her coffee and took a long swig, each time she forgot it had become tepid. She screwed up her face in disgust, then looked out of the window as the squall of rain hit the already dirty window, like a power hose. A dismal outlook she thought. DC Steve Hayes arrived looking very worried. He told his boss about the witness who was now on holiday in Florida with his wife and children. She just glared at him, he found himself on the verge of melt down and demotion. He couldn't remember what he'd told the witness last night as it was his first suspicious death and he had felt a little overwhelmed. He realised his mouth had gone dry but didn't want his boss to see him swallow or lick his lips, it's a sign that police officers always look for when questioning.

'What time was the flight?' she asked, still glaring at Steve.

'Um, six thirty to Orlando,' he looked at the office clock and said, 'been flying for four hours now.'

'Then as a witness, who has already given a statement and has not been arrested or charged therefore there are no bail conditions, what is the next procedure, DC Hayes?' she said a little too sarcastically.

'Wait 'til the witness returns, which is next Saturday?' He gave a half smile, gauging his boss's expression.

'Correct.' Then she picked up her mug of stone cold coffee, took a swig and spat it back in disgust, and at the same time splatters landed on Jim Crosby's statement before her. Steve gave her a smirk as she took a quick look around at the rest of the team but no one had seemed to notice her. She gave Steve a half smile.

During the late afternoon Steve was assigned telephone duty. Julie couldn't help but notice how pleased he was during the last phone call, his voice became a little louder and clearer as if he wanted the rest of the team to hear him. She liked him, as he didn't take offence and had a dry sense of humour. The CID department was still waiting for the promotions to go through, she was sure he wouldn't be on the list as he needed more experience especially with suspicious deaths and procedures.

Steve looked over to her desk as if reading her thoughts and she glanced back down onto the actions she was reading through when he came over to her desk and said, 'I've just been on the phone to the deceased's aunt, she said she thought her niece had a psychiatric problem of some sort, psychopathic tendencies,' he went on, 'and rarely showed concern with anything. Also she liked to be in control and the aunt wondered if it was something to do with her childhood experiences.' Steve paused, 'apparently the aunt's brother, the deceased's father, had been violent towards the mother, then abandoned his daughter and wife, for a new life elsewhere. Not to be heard from again.'

'Oh right. So had the deceased lived with the aunt?' Julie asked.

'Yes from the age of twelve. A few years later mother died possibly from after effects of the beatings, it was never proven. Then at eighteen, Sara went into nurse training and lived in.'

'Did she keep in contact?'

'Birthdays, Christmas and strangely, Chinese New Year, that's it,' Steve said proudly.

'Chinese New Year?' Julie gave a frown, 'Strange…'

'Yes her mother was Chinese Mandarin.' At that, the desk phone rang, which startled both the detectives, it was the forensic pathologist.

Julie put the phone on loud speaker so her team could listen in.

'Ok Adam what do we have?' Julie said.

'Well, Julie her death was caused by an overdose of an anaesthetic induction agent called Propofol and inhalation sevoflurane,' he paused, 'there are restraining marks on her upper arms and there is peri-mortem bruising on and around her face, which includes the canthus region, maxillary and mandible areas along with two large finger indentations under the mandible.'

'What's the canthus?' Asked Steve.

'Centre part of the face where the nose and eyes meet.' Adam said.

'So what do you suppose caused all the bruising?' asked Julie.

'Force, of course!' said Adam. Then he went on to suggest that a large adult anaesthetic mask had been used hence the large bruised area on the face and that it wasn't suicide, she had been killed.

The MCT incident room became a hive of activity as now they were investigating a murder. The atmosphere became charged with enthusiasm even the permanently tired were sitting alert to what their DI was discussing on the board. Pencils could be heard clicking on teeth or scratching away on paper or in note books, as each team member concentrated. Chief Superintendent Defoe was happy with the way the investigation was being conducted and wanting a step by step update. Julie turned to Steve and said. 'Right Steve you and I are off to the deceased's house to see if we can find any more clues. Steve felt his head swell as he passed DS Moni Reece who clicked her teeth with her pencil whilst watching him leave with the DI.

*

The garden gate banged shut as Steve past through, he moved his fingers in case they got caught but the gate was harmless and on close inspection, he noticed its rusty coiled spring was in need of some oil. It wasn't stiff to open but it was due to the lack of compression within that stopped it from reaching its full opening arc. Its firm recoil propelled it shut hence its clatter. Somehow it seemed incongruous to its surroundings and once inside the property it was even more so.

The only sound on entering the house was the hum of the fridge freezer, nothing else. There were no unpleasant odours like old cooking, disinfectant, kitchen drain smells or pets as this was a main concern. Basically the house was pristine clean, no out of date food in the fridge and what was in there had been wrapped carefully or in containers. It could be a holiday rental but for the pricey looking ornaments and photos dotted around.

The upstairs rooms were equally pristine clean and in each of three bedrooms, not a thing out of place. The duvet covers had been painstakingly ironed and smoothed down, not a crease in sight. Even the bathroom and en-suites were presented as perfect, all tiles floor to ceiling were shining as if polished with not a speck of dust to be seen. To Steve it appeared that an obsessive cleaner, probably with OCD lived here. He did a search through each room for anything that could be useful and came across a drawer full of sexy underwear, Ann Summers style. Each item had been folded neatly and colour coded, red, gold, yellow, blue, silver, pink, purple and white. No black, unusual thought Steve. In the next drawer down there was standard underwear and socks that Steve thought were probably for work.

On hearing his boss busy downstairs he left the room and went back down to join her.

'Nothing to note upstairs, only a drawer full of sexy underwear!' he said.

'Give you a thrill, did it Steve?' she laughed and continued searching the writing bureau and pulled out some paints then said, 'An artist perhaps?' She held out the tray for Steve to see, 'Acrylics and several different colours.'

'Strange, those colours are similar to some of the under wear.' Steve said.

Julie took out the computer and gave it to Steve to hold while she continued exploring the bureau. She closed the lid and went over to the chiffonier and opened the top drawer and got a waft of some floral scent. Within the next drawer down, there were five empty Nokia phone boxes laying in a row. Each had numbers and animal characters painted on the front. Inside each empty box there was a collection of colours, numbers and symbols clearly done by someone who had artistic calligraphy skills, Chinese perhaps?

'We'll take these items with us too, forensics have finished here,' she said as she piled them up on the top of the chiffonier. 'Any sign of her mobile phone yet, Steve?'

'No, the forensics took a look in Sara's handbag last night and couldn't see anything, no purse not even an address book but did find a receipt.'

'Sara would've used her mobile to store phone numbers, just wish we could find it. She didn't like litter, untidiness or waste, she was organised. I feel she was a paper free, save the trees sort of person,' Steve said.

'I don't think she was a save the tree's sort, I think she had a form of OCD and disliked any form of hoarding, so paper free makes more sense, apart from this receipt?'

'Yeah, from a take-away in Henfield, China House and it was for the amount of fifteen pounds and seventy pence,' said Steve.

'Ah what was ordered?'

'Numbers two, six, ten and nineteen and the date was November twentieth this year.'

'Long way to go for a Chinese meal. There's lots of take-away restaurants nearby,' Julie said, 'I think we'll give them a call on the way to Emily Lewis's place, in Henfield.

*

The office smelt like a canteen, with a variety of fast foods sitting on each desk and the hungry occupants stuffing their faces as if it would be their last meal. Someone had placed an unopened Chinese chow mein on Julie's desk and when she spotted it she gave them all a smile and thumbs up as they knew better than to leave her out.'We need to regroup and share what we have now,' Julie said and when she saw their faces, '- well after lunch then.'

20

It was the sound of crunching gravel that made Emily look up from her book. David didn't move he just continued to read his newspaper instead gave a grunt in acknowledging the sound but that was all. Emily glanced over at him half hoping he would go and see who it was but he didn't budge, he could be a lazy bastard at times, she thought. Then she tutted him as she reluctantly stood and made her way over to the window, moved the curtain and peeped outside. It was still raining and the car's headlights glistened and sparkled as the driver straightened up. She didn't recognise who it was at first until the occupants stepped out of the car, pulled up their coat collars and walked briskly up to the front door. The front door bell rang. David skimmed a quick look over at her and grimaced to let her know he had no intention of answering it. She rolled her eyes at his bowed head and left the room to answer the door.

David could hear voices at the open door which were partially drowned out by the rain but then the tone changed as the front door closed, obviously Emily had invited them in, whoever they were. He felt mildly annoyed at having unplanned visitors, especially on a Sunday evening. Don't they have a home to go, he thought? Then the living room door swung opened and Emily hurried in wearing an anxious expression, this made him put down his newspaper.

'What's the matter darling?' he said more irritated than concerned.

She didn't reply immediately, and as two solemn people followed her into the living room, she introduced them. David stood unsure if he should shake their hands but then decided it wasn't the done thing, especially as they were introduced as the Major Crime Team, MCT. There had been a suspicious death at the hospital, one of the staff, so David quickly excused himself leaving Emily and the two detectives alone.

'Please sit down,' she said as she motioned them to a large sofa.

'Thank you. I'll get to the point Mrs Lewis. The death of Sara Eaton is now being treated as murder,' said Julie who studied Emily's reaction to this news, 'and we have a few questions and requests.'

'Perhaps my husband should be present, as he is a solicitor, well he was until his sudden redundancy from a law firm.'

'His presence won't be necessary. Which law firm?

'Byrne, Radcliffe & Lewis, he was a partner there. . .' Emily said dismissively. 'All this is terrible…awful… 'I'll need to inform the Chief Executive, Daphne Warren.' Emily fidgeted with her hands as her colour drained from her face. Steve knew this NHS manager didn't like Sara and that this reaction could be due to feelings of shame, or perhaps she knew more.

'Yes and please do that preferably before the press get wind of this news?' Said Julie.

Steve noticed the discarded newspaper and noted the headline, Brexit; Article Fifty end of March 2017.

Julie and Emily started to speak at the same time, Emily motioned for her to continue.

'We'll need names of all the staff in your department, their rotas, days off, annual leave, sickness, study leave etc. ,' said Julie, 'also any locums, agency staff, maintenance, reps, laundry, CSSD and any other possible visitors to your department.'

As Emily wrote a memo Julie said, 'Tonight I would like all the names you can supply. If you can access them on line or perhaps you may need to go back to the hospital. I'll leave you to choose,' then added, 'there will be police scene guards in the hospital so I'll let them know you may be in. Please follow our rules not to contaminate the area cordoned off.'

Julie looked at Steve and said, 'Do you want to ask any questions DC Hayes?'

'Yes. Did Sara have any close friends or enemies?

'Um…well…neither,' Emily sighed as she avoided eye contact by looking around, 'not that I know of…' her voice trailed off as if in deep thought.

'Did you get on with Sara?' Steve asked.

'I'm a manager first, I don't need to work with the staff as such,' Emily said eyes flicking back and forth as if put out by the mere question, 'I didn't like Sara much that's true, she was quiet and pushy at times. She appeared friendlier with some of the male staff…'

'What do you mean, male staff?' asked Steve who was now becoming confident in his new role.

'She err... flirted.'

'That's not unusual for a good looking single woman to do?'

'She had a...well, like a hold on them...strange.' Emily gave another sigh this time irritated.

Julie decided to change tactics, as the living room door opened and David Lewis entered, he smiled at his wife and said. 'Well is everything okay? All done?'

'Sara Eaton was murdered David.' Emily said now near to tears. He quickly made his way over to her side and he slipped an arm around her shoulders, as a comforting gesture.

'She was such a flirt...I wonder if that had something to do with her...' Emily stopped herself then David nodded in agreement as he hugged his wife.

'Seems Sara was a one for the men, huh?' he said in a half sneer. Steve noticed a fleeting look of puzzlement in the wife's eyes as she stiffened slightly.

'Anyway how did she die?' David went on.

'Can't disclose that information Mr Lewis.' Said Julie as she stood followed closely by Steve.

She didn't move for a moment then looked down at her feet and touched her forehead with two fingers as if in thought, reminiscent of the TV character Detective Colombo. The room was silent waiting for her to say something. Then just as Colombo would do, she grimaced and looked up to Emily then David.

'We found a receipt dated twentieth of November, belonging to the deceased, for a Chinese take-away meal in Henfield, it's a mystery to us as there are so many nearer take-aways in Worthing.'

'Lots of people have take-away meals. Why should that be a mystery, Detective Inspector?' David said aggressively.

'A mere observation Mr Lewis,' said Julie, 'we have to follow up any possible leads.'

'Leads?'

'It's police procedure to check out anything that could be of help in this case,' Julie said as she kept eye contact with him, 'surely you must be aware of that being a solicitor?'

As the two detectives got into their unmarked police car, Julie sat for a few seconds and started to tap the steering wheel rhythmically which mildly irritated Steve.

'I wonder how he knew that she was a one with the men,' said Julie, then her phone pinged an incoming message, it was Harry wondering when she'd be home for dinner. She knew she'd be wrapped up in this case and wished Harry would just let her get on. She sent an abrupt reply and almost wished she hadn't, but too late, it had gone.

'Yeah,' said Steve looking ahead at the rain pelting down on the car's front window screen and added, 'arrogant little critter isn't he?'

'Well he is a solicitor, aren't they all like that?'

The cold fresh breeze buffeted its way in to the hallway as Emily stood watching the detectives drive off. Rain lashed down as if from a high powered hose and with each gust of wind the droplets would whirl around confused, as if the imaginary hose had become unevenly clogged. She became mesmerized by it all as her thought went back to that odd meal delivery about a week ago. Now what date was the kitchen fire she thought? Then shivered as she shut the door?

David had his head in the newspaper and didn't say anything as she entered the living room. It annoyed her as he tended to be dismissive of events past and present.'Oh for God's sake David at least you could say something, Sara one of my staff nurses has been murdered!'

'What am I supposed to say then...huh?'

'Well there was no need to bad mouth her in front of those detectives,' she said more calmly, 'but I'm intrigued at this Chinese meal?'

'Oh please stop trying to solve other people's problems, Em. You know how upset it makes me just to think of that kitchen fire!' he said firmly.

'What are you saying? There was something in it, that meal arriving?'

'I never said anything of the sort. It was just a coincidence, that's all.'

She studied her husband's face assiduously then he dropped his eyes back to his reading and shook his paper straight that annoyed her, too.

*

Emily was pleased she'd got that phone call out of the way. The Chief Executive Daphne Warren had this habit of trivialising and patronising people and Emily imagined her in a cocktail dress entertaining her cronies.

'Do keep me updated with events Emma.' Daphne Warren said.

'Yes I will and my name is Emily not Emma. Thank you,' Emily said and hung up.

21

The initial investigation was a struggle to piece together with all information, small or irrelevant, to be treated as vital evidence. The paper actions were mounting already, one led to another load of actions that seem to cascade into more, much like a spider's web.

Julie sat at her desk staring at the rain-lashed window stifling yet another yawn, she was tired and needed to get some sleep. The loud ringing from her desk phone took her by surprise, she gave a small shriek as her heart thumped like the base beat of nearby music. She answered it immediately and wondered if the caller DC Will Partis noticed the shocked surprise in her voice. He was up for promotion and Julie felt he deserved it as he was a thorough detective who knew how to follow leads, like a blood hound, she smiled to herself. Yes if there was anything he thought was crucial, he'd phone it in. Like now.

'Ma'am, I've found that one of the doctors from the hospital had been arrested, without charge, for disorderly conduct, about six weeks ago.' Will said.

'Where was this arrest?'

'In the same road where the murder victim lived, in fact just outside the house.'

'Had he been drinking?'

'No. There had been a report of someone lurking around in a back garden. The attending officers said he was distressed about something and reluctant to share it. Apparently he was becoming aggressive and refusing to go home so they decided to arrest him for breach of the peace,' added Will, 'he was released early the next morning, very apologetic. A patrol car dropped him back to his car, outside the murder victim's house.

'Okay, so was there anything noted by that officer?'

'Yes, there was a Smart Car, registration checked out to belong to a Mrs Janie Clarke, a florist in Goring… I have her address so I'll call round there now, should be in on a Sunday.'

'Good work Will, I'll leave you on that action,' Julie hung up, made a few notes then addressing the office said, 'I need someone to follow up a doctor…,' her eyes fell on Detective Sergeant Monica Reece. Moni looked up and smiled at her boss.

'You want me to go somewhere on an action?' Moni said as she put down her pencil.

'Yes Moni,' Julie said, 'the doctor- his name is Owen Muller works at the Western Sussex hospital. See if he knew Sara Eaton.'

Moni stood and beckoned to Steve.

*

The relentless rain was a depressing sight, everywhere there were puddles like small lakes and even the confused street lamps had flickered on. Their reflection on the wet surfaces was more akin to the work of an impressionist at work. Will found Mrs Clarke's house set back off the road. Its short driveway was ideal for a Smart Car, there was a convenient space by the front door that appeared waterlogged from the constant rain. He knew someone was at home as the front room light was on and the blinds were wide open which allowed him a good look in to the room. It looked a wreck with newspapers and clothing strewn around the place. The condensation building up on the windows looked like some cooking was in progress.

Will pulled up his collar against the rain as he pressed the old dull cream doorbell that he heard faintly somewhere within the house. He waited for what seemed like a couple of minutes, then the door opened. A man in his late thirties unshaved and unkempt stood with a disinterested look on his face then in a glum voice the man asked what Will wanted.

'Sorry to bother you sir but I'm investigating an incident where a car belonging to a Mrs Janie Clarke was mentioned,' Will said at the same time showing his identity badge.

The man just stared at the detective then said, 'What do you want to know?'

Will wondered if the couple had just rowed.' May I speak to Mrs Clarke please sir?'

'I'm afraid you're too late, she died on the seventeenth of November… just gone.'

Will was shocked at this revelation, dead, how? He gave his condolences and apologised for intruding on the man's grief. But he had to ask some more questions it seemed cold blooded. It wasn't appropriate at that moment to say it was a murder enquiry. Then he reiterated why he was there as it was crucial to an investigation. Alan invited him in to the hall out of the rain.

'It was just that one of our patrol cars had noted that a Smart Car belonging to your late wife was parked outside a house in Rosemary Drive on the fourteenth of November?' Alan looked away then focused on the coats hanging up in front of him.

'No idea, probably one of her friends, she had so many. She was a florist…she was my wife.' He shook his head dejectedly at the floor.

'Would you know a Sara Eaton?'

Alan kept his head low and eyes down cast. No way was he going to admit he knew that bitch, no way, he thought. 'No… no,' he said. Will noticed the hesitation then thanked Alan Clarke for his time and left him to his grieving.

Will sat looking out of his unmarked police car, his breath soon started to mist up the glass interior that just made a more dismal view of the street. His phone pinged a message it was Steve, wondering if he was finished with the Smart Car investigation. Will didn't reply immediately as he was still thinking of the conversation and body language of Alan Clarke.

Within minutes, the front door opened and Alan Clarke emerged garbed in leather, carrying a motor bike crash helmet. He swiftly made his way to his garage, Will was pleased with the effect of the misted windows.

Now wearing his crash helmet Alan wheeled out his motor bike, pulled it on its stand, turned its ignition and fired it up. The engine had a powerful roar and Will imagined speeding up the motor way in the outside lane, leaving every one behind in its wake.

Alan mounted his motor bike and sped away unaware that he was being followed by the detective all the way to Rosemary Drive. He parked his bike took off his helmet and carried it under his arm as he walked slowly up the path to Sara's house. Then he gently tapped on the glass panel in the centre of the door, the type with a bubble effect that can distort a face. He looked about and up to the bedrooms, then glimpsed into the front room window. He tapped the window and waited and waited. His hair was now slick with rain and every so often he would wipe his hand over it as if to mangle out the wet. No one answered the door. Good he thought.

The unmarked police car was misted up again but that was okay, Will had seen what he wanted and wondered if Alan was aware of Sara's murder and what was his connection to her?

Alan needed to get his stuff from Sara's bathroom, he was overcome with remorse and just wanted to get his stuff and dump it. He didn't want a constant reminder of his infidelity. He cursed himself for not bringing his car keys as they had Sara's door key on it. Shit he muttered under his breath. The relentless rain splashed and trickled down his neck and made him shiver. At that moment he thought of Janie and wanted to cry. He remembered how they bickered when he got home late on that rainy day.

Reluctantly he put his helmet back on and left the house heading towards his bike. As he looked up he noticed the same Mondeo that was parked outside his house earlier, which was now parked across the road. He stood for a few moments pretending to fumble with his gauntlet gloves. He kept his head down but he looked up through his wet eye lashes to observe, he knew someone was inside as the windows were so misted up. He certainly wasn't going over to take a look. He got on his motor bike, started it up and sped off home, it could wait for another day.

Will thought it could all be innocent that Alan had found the house number somewhere in his late wife's address book. If Sara had been his late wife's friend he may be concerned about her plight. Sometimes a little paranoia is a good thing when investigating a case, yet Will felt there was a connection and decided to return to the office. He quickly sent a message to Steve, that he was on his way back with some progress.

The office door seemed permanently open, allowing a cold breeze to whisk in which was unwelcomed in the winter especially if it has been raining all day. The only real invite was the aroma of coffee, it took ages to get this espresso machine up and running. Someone got it from Tesco a "De'Longhi Dedica," that could hold up to four cups at a time, just perfect for the office. It had been on the filing cabinet in its box for almost a month, then someone took it out of the box and it stayed there waiting for attention for a further two weeks. Then one fine morning someone had got it up and running and the coffee kept on coming. The first place to visit when back in the office was the espresso machine.

As soon as Will got back to the office he found Steve and told him what he had found out so far. Steve lacked Will's confidence and sometimes he felt envy especially when his boss gave so much time to him. Steve watched as Will went into Julie's office, smarmy git he thought. Her door was always open but Steve still knocked. She looked up and smiled at him and beckoned him in to sit on a small cabinet next to Will who was already comfortable in a chair opposite. She put down her pen, then leaned back in her chair to listen to what he had found out.

'It may not be anything but the owner of the Smart Car died on the seventeenth of November, two days after it was spotted outside Sara Eaton's house. Her husband thought Sara Eaton may be a friend of his late wife,' said Will, then reported the rest of his investigation on the husband.

'That's good work Will,' she said, impressed, as they came out to the incident board. Steve joined them and asked where the husband worked. Both Julie and Will looked at him in surprise. Will knew how much Steve wanted to out shine him, he remembered once feeling like that when he first joined the MCT. He smiled to himself.

'Would you like me to run a check on him ma'am?' said Steve trying to sound efficient in front of Will.

'Good idea, I'll leave that to you Steve,' said Julie and went back to looking at the board. Will gave Steve a nod as if to say well done.

The civilian staff were at their disposal especially for further enquiries so Steve requested a more thorough search on Alan Clarke and interestingly found he worked at the Western Sussex Hospital, the Worthing site and couldn't wait to share his news.

'Okay, so what have we got so far?' said Julie to her team when her desk phone started to ring. She rolled her eyes as she went over to answer it. 'DI Robertson,' she said abruptly.

'Julie, you've not replied to my text or phone messages!' Harry snapped. 'You hate me phoning on this line but at least I can speak to you!'

Julie moved around her desk to sit down and spoke quietly to her husband as the team pretended to be busy. 'I'm sorry Harry, I haven't even switched it on sorry.' She spoke calmly.

'What... I've actually wasted all this time phoning a switched off phone? Suppose I'd taken ill or something?'

'Yeah... you're right but you've got me now. Are you okay?' she said, whispering into the phone.

'Oh for God's sake, you sound like some bloody spy!'

'This is a murder inquiry Harry, and you know it means I'm....'she was about to say something else when she heard some bleeping sounds in the back ground. 'Are you alright Harry...where are you?' She said it loud enough for the Steve to hear, and he looked over to her in her office.

'A&E. Chopped my bloody finger off, waiting for a surgeon to sew it back on under G. A.'

'Oh my God Harry, how did you do that?'I'll be right there darling. . . I'll be right there.' She ended the call and as she switched on her mobile phone she called for a quick hand over meeting to DS Moni Reece, 'Moni let Defoe know that I've had to leave suddenly, Harry is in A&E…' she said, trying to sound in control but her moist eyes told another story. 'He's only gone and chopped off his finger!'

22

Even before the Chinese take-away restaurant had opened its doors the smell of food stirred up the rumblings in Steve's stomach. He wished he'd phoned ahead and ordered a sweet and sour with fried rice, he imagined it in its foiled container sealed by a waxed cardboard lid, waiting to be peeled back. He tried to remember when he last ate a decent meal, was it yesterday he thought? Had he eaten with his wife or had he been dreaming it, whatever, he couldn't remember exactly.

Moni paced back and forth looking at her watch in the hope that the staff behind the counter in the take-away read her impatient body language. 'If they don't open these bloody doors soon I'll have to knock on the window,' she said, exasperated with the wait, 'Christ why do they have to open at the precise time?'

'Just show your warrant card, that always works,' Steve said, a little cockily. Moni gave him a sharp look then smiled.

'You hungry Steve?'

'Bloody sure I am, if I don't eat soon I'll start to dribble.'

'We'll grab chips from that chippy next door to the undertakers when we're finished here.'

'Not very nice - a chippy next door to an undertakers.' Steve scorned.

They both turned back at the sound of the door being unlocked, it opened and they both walked in. The man at the counter looked from Steve to Moni and asked for their order. Moni pulled out her warrant card and prompted Steve to do the same. Then she slid a photo of a smiling Sara Eaton holding what looked like a scroll, over the counter for the man to study.

'Have you ever seen this woman, a customer perhaps?' Moni asked quietly.

'No I don't think so,' he said, after studying the photo. ' I'll ask my sister.' He turned to a woman who had just finished taking a telephone order. She smiled at her brother then at Moni and looked hard at the photo.

'Yes I've seen her a few times in here, last time was…' she stopped to think, 'um, not sure but quite recently.'

'I have a receipt here with a date on it, if that would help you?' said Moni.

The woman took the receipt and nodded a yes, 'It was a delivery meal, let me check the diary and I'll let you know for sure,' she said.

'Also we need to know who it was delivered to, please,' said Steve.

'Ah here we are,' the woman tapped the page as she passed it over to Steve, 'it was for the Lewis' place just outside Henfield on the way to Partridge Green.' Then she added, 'I remember they phoned us later to tell us they hadn't ordered it, it was a mistake. I told the man that the lady,' she pointed at the photo of Sara Eaton, 'had ordered and paid for it and given his address.'

Steve asked the woman if they could buy some chips but they were in the fryer still and would take at least fifteen minutes. Clearly he was hungry and Moni steered him out to the nearby fish & chip shop along the road next to the undertakers for their take away lunch. When they got back to the car they sat quietly eating from the paper package, the smell of fish, chips and vinegar reeking within their Ford Mondeo.

23

Although unpredictable, it was generally quieter at the weekends, but the work at that moment on ITU was just as intense as a week day. This was where Owen preferred to work, not in elective surgery. Here each patient posed a challenge- after all, some were very ill. He continued his round to each bed reviewing prescription charts occasionally altering doses or adding more medication.

Most of the patients were unconscious and were unable to confirm they were nil-by-mouth, and reliant upon the sign which hung above their bed. Yet the housekeeper, along with his well-stocked trolley of water jugs and scratched plastic tumblers would still exchange the earlier untouched delivery. Following that the cleaning would take place which irritated Owen to distraction, especially when a fluffy mop appeared over his shoulder and up to the screen's rail then over the top of a vulnerable patient. In response Owen tutted and sighed, hoping this would have some effect on the housekeeper to hasten his chore. Other staff were diligently caring for their patients and smirked at Owen's reaction as the fluffy mop did one last swoop – even the housekeeper gave a smile.

*

Each time Moni went down to the basement to the police garage for a pool vehicle, she noticed that there was always one particular treasure available. This unmarked police car, a Ford Mondeo, was a bit of a wreck, not only had it been driven into but it had driven into something too. It was road worthy, safe and at least it got them from place to place. Still she had a job to do and was pleased when Steve joined her for this particular action. He volunteered to drive them to Owen Muller's place in Henfield, a growing village in west Sussex.

The huge detached Victorian house stood about one hundred yards from the road. It was separated by a Common, Henfield Common which was a conservation area for wildlife, and was carefully managed by the parish. Moni pressed the door bell and waited, usually it could be heard ringing somewhere in the house but there was only silence, she wondered if it worked at all. She pressed it again and listened carefully, she thought she heard a faint barking but that was all. She took a tentative look into the front double bay windows and noted the smart classic décor, something she would never be able to afford.

Steve stood back watching her antics, then he suggested that perhaps they should ask one of the neighbours. Then at that moment a car pulled up, a grey haired man in his fifties got out, shut the car door and walked up the garden path towards the two detectives. He frowned then hesitated to speak and when he did speak it was an educated voice, the sort of accent from a privileged, private school. Posh, thought Moni.

'Can I help you? asked the grey haired man.

'Yes sir, we're looking for Doctor Owen Muller,' said Moni not wanting to give anything away.

'May I ask who you are?' At that Moni and Steve took out their warrant cards which the grey haired man took and studied carefully before returning them. The two detectives stood patiently waiting for him to speak. 'Thank you detectives but Dr Muller is at work and will not be home until later.'

'Who are you sir?' asked Steve whilst standing in the porch for shelter from the drizzle.

'I am,' he said in a condescending voice, 'Dr Crawford, Consultant Anaesthetist, detective constable.'

'Why are you here Dr Crawford?' asked Moni.

'Actually I'm here to let Wallace out for a pee,' and chuckled, 'he's a dog, don't worry.'

Moni smiled, she had thought she'd heard a dog somewhere in the house earlier.

'Nothing serious I hope?' Dr Crawford said.

'Just some routine questions, we'll come back later.' Said Steve.

'I'll let him know… I'll see him later when I take over from him in ITU at Worthing Hospital.'

*

It was nearing five pm, Owen felt his stomach rumble he had missed lunch again. If he didn't take care he'd end up with an ulcer… too much knowledge he thought. Yet he had no real appetite since Laura left him. He felt he'd taken a nose dive in his life. If I end up with an ulcer then that serves me right for being such a bastard, he thought.

The continual rhythmic sound of the bleeps alarmed at intervals and would alert the staff nurses to their patients' needs, to change intra venous solutions and medication. It was the intermittent noise from suctioning that reminded Owen of his own father attempting to drink hot soup from a spoon. He smiled at that thought.

Owen looked at the clock, almost time for hand over to Leonard and he hoped he wouldn't be late. He rubbed his stomach to try and stop the noisy rumbling. The thoughts of a large whiskey and of Laura popping round later lifted his mood, at least they were on calm talking terms now. He didn't want to create any more problems, only to show her that now he was a reformed person, learned his lesson. How he missed them, being a family again.

There was the usual strong smell of coffee in the office. The recent aroma was enough to cause salivation, even for the non-coffee drinkers a bit like the effect of fried bacon on a vegetarian, a strange concept. Also it made the office feel more cosy and welcoming even though cold. Steve sat down at his desk and surveyed his colleagues, he'd just got back from Henfield and wished he'd bought a take away coffee from the garage in Golden Square. His DS was busy talking to the boss, who returned to the evidence board and started to discuss connections. Steve was eager to join in and view the scanty evidence so far. He suggested a late return visit to Henfield to see Dr Muller and to his surprise, they agreed.

'We'll need to run a check on Dr Crawford, see if there's anything on him,' said Moni, 'might have to check his credentials on the hospital web site first...although he looked kosher.

*

Owen wasn't sure what time Laura would turn up so the first thing he did when he entered his empty house was to fuss over Wallace, let him out, put food in his dish, pour a large whiskey for himself then head for the shower.

He looked around the living room, then groaned and grimaced at his untidiness that resembled a ransacked jumble sale, the mess would take an army to tidy. He shook his head as he glimpsed himself in the hall mirror, yep definitely an Owen Wilson look-a-like. He ran his fingers through his hair like a comb then took a sip of his whiskey and smiled.

The bathroom didn't look much better, it was as if an entire football team had been in there and it was now in need of a deep clean. He finished his shower and quickly dried himself when he noted the pubic hairs that littered the floor, bath and toilet rim and feeling disgusted he grabbed a stale smelling towel that he had been using all week or possibly two, wiped down the toilet then used the towel as a broom sweeping and flapping the floor debris away from vision.

He topped up his glass, shrugged at the measure then almost in a vault he hurled himself on to the sofa. Lying stretched out he piled cushions under his head, picked up the TV remote and selected BBC news. He didn't hear the car door shut or the key in the lock, he was surprised when he heard his wife's voice. 'Owen are you asleep,' she said as she walked over to him, 'I did knock first just in case you had company.' He ignored her tone and got up to welcome her with a kiss. She allowed him a peck on the cheek that was a step in the right direction he thought, now aware of his own whiskey breath.

'How are the children? I miss them…and you,' he said then, 'have you eaten?'

'No but we could get a take-away from the High Street,' she said cheerfully, then seriously added, 'I miss you too, so do the children.'

He moved towards her, noticing her eyes glistening with tears. They were jolted back to reality as the door bell rung. He shook his head in disbelief and gave her a wry smile.

'Saved by the bell…' she said looking at him through her eye lashes.

'I'll tell you what, Mrs Muller, you order that Chinese take-away and I'll answer the door.'

Owen looked from one to the other, a woman and a man who stood looking at him and at first he thought they were, Jehovah's Witnesses or Mormons. When they introduced themselves and showed their ID, they said they'd called round earlier and spoke to a Dr Crawford. Owen invited them in and scratched his head then said. 'Yes my colleague said you'd been round earlier. Is there some problem?'

'We are investigating a very serious crime, sir…eh…Dr Muller,' Moni said.

'Oh what's happened?' Owen asked anxiously.

At that moment Laura came back in to the sitting room, looking concerned as she sat down next to her husband.

'Where were you on the night of the fourteenth of November?' Moni asked because the police computer system had flagged his name and caution as he had been arrested for breach of the peace outside Sara Eaton's house, and she wondered if there was a connection.

Laura stood, 'I'll get your desk diary, Owen,' she said and disappeared out to his study, on return she was flitting through the diary like an efficient secretary, 'Ah… well… not a good day by the looks.'

Owen took the diary, where he had entered, *Laura and the children went to her parents.* 'Oh yes…yes my wife and I had a row and she left me, took the children with her,' he said.

'And who are you madam?' asked Moni, looking at Laura.

'I'm Laura, Owen's wife, we're hoping to get back together at some stage.' Laura said quietly.

'Was there anyone else you went to see that night Dr Muller?' Steve asked.

'No. I was here, upset.'

'We note on our police records that you were arrested on that night of the fourteenth of November and charged with breach of the peace. You spent a night in a cell to cool off and were let off with a caution. So it appears that you did go out that particular night, sir…err doctor.' Moni looked at her notes then back up to Owen. 'According to the arresting police officer you had stated that you had a falling out of some kind with one of the residents in this road and that left you agitated. Why were you in Rosemary Road in the first place?'

Laura sat back away from Owen, both detectives noticed this move. The doctor turned to his wife and spoke to her first. 'Laura, you were packing to leave me, I was furious that she came here, it was spiteful of her, you know that. I'm sorry but I drove off to her place to have it out with her. She was out and I….' Laura looked at him incredulously.

'Who were you visiting in that road, Dr Muller?' asked Steve.

'It just so happened to be the same road as a colleague…I once had an affair and…I had a row with another motorist, that's all…I didn't see her!'

Both detectives were already aware the victim's neighbour had reported an intruder in the back garden of one of the houses and that it was a man shouting obscenities. The police officer who returned Dr Muller that morning noted the doctor's car was parked outside number forty-two, the victim's house.

'Your colleague's name please?' Steve asked just as his stomach let out a loud groan that everyone heard and chose to ignore.

'Sara Eaton, we work together.'

Moni noticed the present tense used but felt there was a cover up, perhaps to appease his wife.

The doorbell rang and Laura got up to answer it. 'It's probably our Chinese take-away delivery,' she said as she rummaged in her large handbag for her purse, it seemed to take ages until she found it then discovered she had no money in it and turned to Owen. He handed her a twenty pound note from his wallet.

'Get a receipt as its cash,' he said.

Steve remembered the receipt from the Chinese take-away a few days ago, possibly the same place he wondered. Then the waft of sweet and sour sauce started to make him slaver a little. He was aware he'd not eaten all day, nor had Moni who watched the food being placed on a table, sighed and continued her questioning.

'Where were you on Friday evening the twenty ninth of November?' Moni asked.

'Why do you want to know?' Laura asked as she flashed a look at her husband who was now shaking his head.

'Laura I'm not seeing her any more, you can be assured of that!' he said adamantly. He faced her and took her hand, she withdrew it slowly then got up to stand by the window. Steve looked up and over to Moni.

'Dr Muller will you please answer my question?'

'I can't remember, I wasn't on duty so I was probably here,' Owen confessed, 'and... probably too much alcohol. That's my usual evening entertainment these days, in between being on call at the hospital.'

'Is there anyone that can verify you were here?'

'No... look why do you want to know?'

'As we have just said, we are investigating a very serious crime.'

'How serious?'

'Murder,' Moni said as she stared at him, 'you have no one to corroborate your whereabouts, you have lied and misled our enquiry therefore Dr Muller I am arresting you....

'Oh my God, Owen, what have you done...?' Laura gasped.

'I've done nothing wrong, nothing, this is a mistake…!' Owen shouted as Moni finished the caution.

'…Anything you do say may be given in evidence.'

24

The sound from the heavy cell doors shutting against their frame echoed out a proclamation of his incarceration. The distant voices of other detainees could be heard not so far off, some were screaming obscenities, denying their crimes or demanding a solicitor.

Owen sat quietly alone with his head in his hands, elbows on his knees and contemplating whether to ring the duty solicitor. It brought back memories of his recent overnight stay at Worthing police station, somehow he felt different then - probably because he deserved to be locked up to calm down. He could never have imagined he'd be in this situation - a Consultant Anaesthetic being treated like a common criminal inside a grotty hovel like this. He noticed a smell and glanced around to a lone toilet in the corner of his nine by six foot space. It had no seat and on the floor nearby was a discarded cardboard inner of a used up toilet roll. He stood up to inspect the toilet more thoroughly and noted the floaters from the previous occupant, and drips of urine lay idle on the sealed flooring around its pedestal. He thought back to his own dirty bathroom and sighed, imagining what Laura would say when she saw his style of housekeeping.

He heard movement by the door then jangling keys and wondered if he was being observed through the little round spy hole within its thick metal access. Suddenly the door swung open and outwards into the corridor and there stood an officer with a friendly smile. His hair was shorn far too short which gave him the appearance of a thug and as he carried the welcoming tray of tea he looked incongruous to his role. The pre packed cake looked more like bread pudding and later proved to be out of date by a month. As the officer handed over the tray he assured Owen that the detectives would be along very soon to carry out their interview. Then the thug officer left the cell and clanged the door shut.

Owen sat back down on the bed and onto its thin mattress which seemed to collapse into a flat state from under his weight. He pondered at the thought of having to sleep on it. He sipped his tea, it wasn't too bad after all just a shame there was nothing else to eat.

It had only been about twenty minutes within this windowless cell with no spare toilet paper...Owen shook his head bleakly at nothing in particular.

*

The Chief Superintendent Defoe paced the floor of his office with his arms crossed and occasionally he'd bring up his hand and with his index finger, tap his mouth, a strange habit he had when concentrating on something. A knock at the door brought him to a standstill where he ran his palm over his slightly balding head, pulled straight his uniform jacket and gave a clearing of his throat as if about to give a speech.

'Come in,' he said curtly and as Julie entered, he invited her to sit in a comfortable seat by the shredder. He probably sat there with unwanted documents and processed their demise whilst watching staff toing and froing from his window thought Julie. 'Update me,' said Defoe.

'DS Moni Reece and DC Steve Hayes have followed a line of enquiry to an Anaesthetist Dr Owen Muller and it turns out he has connection to the deceased.'

'What's that?'

'The doc had an affair with the deceased, no alibi for the night of her death and has withheld important information,' Julie sighed, 'DS Reece has arrested him for further questioning.

'Do you think that is a wise move, Julie?' Defoe made an expression like a boxer dog, chin out and mouth drooping downwards. Julie knew from the past that when he made that expression it was disapproval.

'It's all we have to go on at the moment, sir.'

'I've read through the desk sergeant's report and you can't assume anything, not enough evidence Julie, not enough. Release him.'

'Bail?'

'Not this soon,' Defoe frowned, 'Speak to DS Reece and DC Hayes about this lack of evidence.' He walked over to the window next to Julie and stood looking out then said, 'Obviously he's more of a person of interest at this stage.' Julie nodded an agreement.

Julie went back to the incident room where the MCT team were busy updating the evidence board. They watched as Julie removed Dr Muller from the arrest group and re stuck him into person of interest. Moni shook her head and said, 'He has something to hide and whatever it is we'll find it.' Julie looked at Moni.

'Release him Moni but keep searching for evidence.' Julie then turned to the team, 'Ok then gather around, it seems Dr Muller is now a person of interest so until we can get evidence on him, he'll remain in that category.' She paused as if mulling over the board, everyone remained quiet waiting for clues. 'So far, we have several connections, Emily Lewis disliked Sara and so it seems, did Emily's husband David. But why didn't he speak favourably? Needs to be looked into, Moni and Steve that's a job for you. Apparently he was a solicitor until recently, a sudden redundancy from Byrne, Radcliffe and Lewis. He was a partner and needs to be investigated… Will, you can do some more searching on Alan Clarke, see what you can come up with there. Myself, I'll visit this Louise Brooks who works in the hospital's theatre, see what she knows and if necessary borrow more CID to go out for further questioning. Anything of interest let me know immediately.'

Julie went into her office and closed her door to, something she didn't often do, she felt a little guilty but then she would feel better knowing how Harry was doing. She felt like a naughty girl as she hunched over her desk phone waiting for him to answer.

'Harry, how are you?' she said in a hushed voice.

'Ah Julie, yes I'm ok…is there a problem?'

'Yes you! I can't stop thinking of your finger and how you're managing,' she said.

'I'm fine, Julie. I've got some help in the kitchen, our neighbour Gina has prepared the food and thank God for that new dishwasher,' Harry said reassuringly. 'Now stop worrying about me, how about you, ETA home?'

'You've got to be kidding Harry!'

'Yes I am, see you when you do get home. Don't worry about me - get that murderer!'

Julie smiled to herself, 'I hope you're not patronising me Harry.'

'Look I'll see you later,' he said and hung up. Julie thought of their Italian neighbour a divorced woman and younger than Julie, I'll have to watch out there, she probably likes to mother, she thought.

*

The old building was probably around eighteenth century and the brass plate by the open door bore the names Byrne, Radcliffe & Lewis. Steve was interested as to why David Lewis was no longer a partner and wondered if some embezzlement was involved. The thought of that brought a smile to his face. David Lewis was an arrogant character who had something to hide, he felt sure of that. Moni listened to her junior's assumption then with a shrug of her shoulders said, 'you can never assume anything in detective work, Steve and believe me I've had my days of assuming, so wait until evidence presents itself or you've developed a copper's nose.'

'Yeah, ok but I just have that feeling,'

They climbed the highly polished staircase that resembled marble, everything in its wake was pristine and expensive. The secretary was first to greet them with a friendly smile which soon changed to a serious look when both Moni and Steve showed their I. D. cards. Her hair had been stacked haphazardly on top of her head as if about to topple - but for the over use of hair pins and spray. It remained sturdy. Her caked on make-up and false eye lashes resembled the Chucky doll which rendered Steve speechless as he looked on incredulously.

'So who would you like to speak to?' The secretary addressed them in a slightly haughty tone.

'The senior partner, will do,' said Moni.

'May I know what this concerns?'

'We are investigating a serious crime and cannot divulge information at this time.'

'Is it something to do with David Lewis?' she said looking down and showing her new lashes.

Both officers said nothing as she fluttered them down to the intercom and pressed a switch to announce their arrival. She invited them to take a seat. Within seconds a harried yet pleasant man appeared introduce himself as Mr Byrne, the senior partner and asked them to follow him back to a large impressive office lined with books on every shelf. The floor space was clearly used as a space for filing with each stack carefully placed. There was a smell of beeswax polish and it came from an enormous glossy desk that did not suggest a muddled mind. Each area had some kind of compartment or receptacle for pencils, pens, paper clips, new writing paper, envelopes and so on. The detectives were politely ushered to two antique - looking Queen Anne chairs whilst Mr Byrne continued to the other side of the huge desk which reflected the window, ceiling lights and Mr Byrne's hand which kept going out to straighten things, a little bit of OCD thought Steve.

'How may I help you?' he said courteously.

'We wondered if Mr Lewis was still a partner with your firm.'

'Why do you want to know this?'

'He told us of his recent redundancy but failed to say why and as we are investigating a serious crime we have an obligation to know.'

'Did he give you permission?'

'As I said we are investigating a serious crime.'

'How serious?' Mr Byrne asked.

'Suspicious death possible murder.'

'David would not kill a spider let alone another human!'

'There is no accusation here, sir, just need to know who we are dealing with.'

'As far as I'm concerned he had been indiscriminate with female clients more than once and it was deemed proper to release him from his partnership. Read into it as you like…he didn't want any further fuss as he is happily married.'

'I see, thank you sir,' said Moni as she rose from her chair. 'Just one other thing, was one of the females a Sara Eaton?'

Mr Byrne looked uncomfortable at that prospect and indicated he had said enough but acknowledged that there was a client of that name at one time. Moni followed with another enquiry: 'So Sara Eaton had been a client here?'

'Yes a divorce.' Mr Byrne stood to see them out. Moni did not move.

'Was this recent?'

'Quite recent, probably around late September early October it was finalised.'

'So was Sara Eaton one of the indiscriminate female clients?'

'I really wouldn't know, I suggest you ask him?'

Both Moni and Steve allowed themselves to be ushered out of the office and back to the Chucky doll secretary; they said their farewells to her and left.

'See Steve never assume anything,' Moni said as she tapped her head.

25

The decorators had started on the kitchen quite promptly after the fire. Emily just wanted to get it all done before Christmas and get the new range oven set up, sort out the cupboards and utensil racks - but first she needed to clear out the drawers from the existing old cabinets. The dominant smell of fresh paint was keener than the stench from the burnt timbers although every so often this still crept through like that of an old bonfire dampened by rain.

As Emily rummaged through the drawers she came across the piece of paper that she had stowed away a while ago. She picked it out and studied its nicely drawn calligraphy, obviously done by someone with these skills yet it was strange that such an effort was put in to it. She wondered if it had fallen out of a supplement, both numbers had an oriental touch, 14?She wondered if it was something to do with David and casually went off in search of him when she heard him on the phone in the living room, and as she entered he gave her a mildly irritated glance.

'I hope that look wasn't aimed at me,' she jested as he ended the call abruptly.

'No love, it was Mark, he phoned to ask me something. He just can't let go of Sara's memory, he who had so desperately wanted to end their marriage,' he shook his head, 'I bent over backwards to get that divorce decree absolute.'

'Don't get so het up David, he's probably feeling some guilt and grieving.'

'He hated her!'

'I don't understand…. It's too confusing, anyway look, I found this piece of paper in the drawer and do you know anything about it?' She passed it to him and as he studied it he looked slightly alarmed she noticed. 'Well do you know anything about it?' She asked again.

'Of course I don't, just some silly numbers,' he said agitated, 'Look Em I'm busy…have some calls to make, ok?'

'Let me remind you it's my day off, and on my day off, I do housework starting in here!'

'Well go and do it then!'

'Fuck you!' she shouted as she angrily slammed the door at his chauvinistic attitude.

He could hear her deliberately bashing around in the distance and wished she'd just leave him alone so he could sort out Mark. That bastard, he thought, wanted to make an example out of him - an experienced solicitor! David decided to confront Mark preferably at his place as he didn't want Emily to know of the affair he'd had with Sara. It would ruin their marriage…and any chances he had left to get another position in a law firm. In his opinion everyone has a price.

Looking out of the bedroom window and down onto the two parked cars, Emily daydreamed for a moment as the fine rain gathered momentum, sticking to the body work like beads of sweat. She heard the front door shut and watched as David made his way out to his car and without looking up he got in and drove off. She felt that something had pissed him off, maybe he just needed to get himself a job and lighten up, it's not like he had any outside stresses now.

*

The imposing conifer hedge guided David up to the large detached 17th century house, where he parked his car at an angle next to Mark's silver BMW. The front door opened abruptly and the hard faced Mark stood glaring at his friend.

'I do wish you'd phone before visiting me, David 'ole boy, I am a busy man you know!' he said caustically.

'What's that supposed to mean, Mark ol' chap?

'What do you want?'

'What are you inferring?'

'Oh come now David, we discussed all this earlier…' Mark said in a slightly dismissive tone.

David lunged at him knocking him back into the hall where they fell to the floor, neither of them knew how to fight, but a fist came out and caught David in the eye and blood spurted out on to the plush cream carpet below. Mark looked horrified at the red stain and for just a second he laid motionless taking in the scene. He imagined a delivery van arriving at any moment, witnessing their fight, God knows what the driver would make of it all.

'For fuck's sake David apply pressure on it…I don't want to permanently stain the carpet!'

They rolled away from each other then David nimbly jumped to his feet with blood now running down his face and started to shout at Mark.'What's your price…eh…everyone has a price, what's yours Mark?'

As Mark rubbed his fist he looked down at his carpet then back up to David, and narrowed his eyes. 'What do you mean, what's my price?' David made a move towards him again and Mark now standing, took a step back, 'if you step back over this threshold David, I'll be forced to call the police!'

David stood at the door pressing his palm over his cut. Blood still trickled down his face as Mark went in search of something to help stem the flow. A coppery smell from the blood made David feel woozy and this time he leant against the door jamb to steady himself. Mark returned with a wad of kitchen towel and a concerned look on his face

'Why has it come to this David…?' he said in almost a whisper.

'You think I had something to do with Sara's death don't you?' David said as he applied more pressure to his face.

'Look…. we've both been involved with her one way or another but you were sly with the affair…'

'Oh come on now…you were divorcing her!'

'Do you regret it?'

'Every bloody day!' David said almost in tears. 'She infiltrated every single part of my life, it was beyond my control!'

'Steady ol' boy, don't want you going all soft on me,' Mark said. 'Come and have a snifter…' The friendly offer was hard to refuse for David, after all, they'd been good mates forever.

'You'd better spray Vanish on your carpet first, blood's awful stuff to remove.'

'And you'd better think of what you will tell Emily about your injury. Once a nurse always a nurse, David. You can't fool her too quickly.'

'That's my affair!'

'Yeah you're pretty good at your affairs!'

'You can stick your snifter where the sun don't shine as far as I'm concerned!' David snarled.

'Oh before you go, just a conundrum for you…my house keeper Rachael spotted Sara's car turn up your drive, day before she died, I think?' Mark revelled at this.

David left feeling how this would stack up against him if anything else was uncovered. He needed to find an excuse for not going home for a few days and turned back to Mark.

'If Emily should phone for me, just say I'm staying for a few more nights, boys' thing, 'til this eye settles?' Mark looked up from his carpet-spraying and smiled at his friend and nodded ok.

26

The phone kept ringing but no one was free to answer it. Each time someone opened the anaesthetic room door the noisy ventilation flaps became active even though for just a few seconds. Emily knew there was toing and froing yet couldn't be bothered to look up. She was tired and far too busy to give anything the time of day since all the staff shortages and Sara's death. Everyone had become subdued and clearly disliked passing the theatre where her body had been found; even though it was still cordoned off with a scenes of crime police officer, the whole place felt violated. The Chief Executive Daphne Warren insisted that Dr Muller be temporarily suspended until the whole incident had been resolved and that the waiting list should not be interrupted.

A knock on the office door made Emily look up, seeing it was Louise, she smiled some relief then beckoned for her to enter and take a seat.

'You are a welcome interruption Louise Brooks,' said Emily with a smile, 'I'll put the kettle on.'

'Sounds like a good idea.' Louise yawned and said, 'Oh such a boring meeting, Emily, how do people survive on the boring?' She laughed for the first time in ages. Since Sara had joined their team there had been so much unhappiness. She just wanted the status quo… back to being a work family again.

Emily put her head in her hands and started to cry and when she looked up her mascara had run down her face, she looked like one of the zombies from Thriller, thought Louise.

'Oh Emily what is the matter?'

'There's too much going on, Louise, at home and work, I feel trapped…'

'You need to get away, have time off.'

'No I must ride the storm, so to speak, David is part of that storm,' she said as she wiped her eyes creating a black streak up the side of her face. 'Something isn't quite right with him, I feel he's hiding something?'

'Well I can't help you there,' Louise said. 'Why don't you go home early tonight?'

Emily looked up and said, 'I've left my phone at home…would you believe…luckily I have my trusty Pay As You Go here…' and without hesitation she started to look through her drawer, found it and noticed there had been a missed call from David. 'How strange!' she said quietly, more to herself, 'this has happened before.' She looked up at nothing in particular but deep in thought.'Actually it was around the time of our kitchen fire!' She went on as if talking to herself.

'What's strange?' Louise asked.

'Well I had a missed call from David last week…and he never mentioned it.' Emily said puzzled.

'Men don't always…follow up something if they have already found the answer.'

Emily scrolled to a message from her sent box, it was for David with numbers one and four, nothing else, just the very same numbers as on that piece of paper she'd found. She looked up at Louise, confused and said, 'There is something odd going on and strangely enough these numbers are part of it.'

'Oh weird,' said Louise sitting forward as if in a conspiracy, 'seems Daniel had numbers texted to him he thought I had sent them from my phone… it looked as if I had sent it to him instead of Lizzie, so he forwarded on to her. Of course I didn't send it in the first place, looks like someone had used my phone and I didn't have my passcode on!'

'Neither do I on this phone,' Emily paused

'I know this sounds awful but could this have been something to do with Sara...?'

'It seems quite innocuous. I really don't know what to say,' she gave a shrug, 'but I'll ask David when I get home - that's if he's in a better frame of mind.' Emily said.

*

It wasn't actually a privilege to park outside the hospital as the yearly cost was astronomical but there was nowhere else to go, unless it was on the road and sometimes the timely walk was a nuisance especially when attending a meeting or pouring with rain. Emily wondered how Louise managed at times without a car. After all she had an excuse for being late something that she was rarely guilty of and she was trustworthy. In a way Emily found her more suitable as deputy manager than Alan.

As Emily sat in her blue Mini car she thought of Alan, it had been almost two weeks since the funeral of Janie and now Sara's death. This was a diversion too many in her life at this precise moment. She shook her head as she recalled the funeral like it was yesterday, the smell of flowers, lilies, evergreen sprays and wreaths. The variety of cakes that had remained mostly untouched, low humming of voices similar to the drone of bees in a hive. Alan, all the while had walked around in a trance as if he'd been hypnotised. She shook herself out of her reverie started the ignition, backed out of her parking space and drove off home.

There was no sign of David's car when Emily turned her car around and reversed into her space. The outside sensor light remained off and there was no light on in the porch, clearly the sensor light had not even been turned on, usually David's job,and now it seemed eerie in the darkness. She got out of her car and stood for a few moments strangely enjoying the damp darkness and listened to the stream in full flow gushing thunderously over what sounded like a newly built beaver dam. It was too dark to negotiate the path except by the sound of gravel crunching under her feet, she walked cautiously as if about to commit a burglary.

She felt a strong craving for a cigarette but knew there were none anywhere in the house. Shit, she thought, always something to piss me off. She realised that she hadn't actually seen David for at least twenty four hours, he'd gone over to Mark's and he told her not to phone him as he needed male company. That meant he wanted to drink Mark's expensive whisky, boys will be boys she reasoned. God knows when he'll be back home and hopefully in a less stroppy mood.

As she opened the porch door there was a note from the decorators saying they were not able to gain access and would be back tomorrow to try again. They left a phone number for contact. She found her mobile phone with some missed calls, voice mail and texts but nothing from David.

She entered her half-finished kitchen opened the fridge took out the new bottle of wine, unscrewed the lid and poured herself a large glass. She loved the sound of the glug each time, from a new bottle. It was cold in the house so she kept her coat on, sat down and said out loud to no one, 'Yes I think I'll finish the bloody lot!' The last meal she'd had was lunch, a bowl of French fries from the hospital canteen, tasteless and expensive. Now she felt ravenous.

She selected a meal from the freezer and as she pierced the plastic membrane then realised she was actually stabbing it, she shrugged her shoulders. She placed the meal in the microwave, four minutes, just long enough to pour another wine, she thought. She shivered at the lack of heat then heard the click on the timer, not long till the place warms up now she thought. She put the radio on low volume to keep her company.

The knock at her front door was probably David being deposited out of a taxi as he had not taken his house key. She switched on the sensor light to get a better view from the living room window and noticed a car she didn't recognise parked next to her car. Her heart started to thump wildly, she felt sick for a moment and realised it was fear. After all she wasn't expecting any visitors. Her mouth became dry and she wondered if she should take a knife with her. She walked down the hall to the door and in the illumination there were outlines of two people. Cautiously she put the door chain on just in case and opened the door to the gap allowed. She felt rather silly peering through like a nosey neighbour but her expression changed when she recognised DS Moni Reece and DC Steve Hayes standing there staring back at her.

'Oh, what can I do for you?' Emily said surprised.

'We'd like to ask you and your husband a few questions,' Moni said, 'may we come in please?'

'Well he's not here and has not been home for at least eighteen hours.'

Moni stood patiently waiting for access. 'Remember Mrs Lewis this is a murder enquiry and we need to ask some question from you too.' Emily slid the chain back and opened the door to let the two officers inside. She ushered them into the living room apologising for the cold, as the clicking of the radiators were in action but not fast enough to heat the large area there. Emily wished David had been home he'd have the log burner going by now. She missed him.

'Where were you on the twenty ninth of November?' Steve launched.

'I was at work till late afternoon.' Emily said without hesitation.

'Can anyone vouch for that?'

'Of course they can, the entire unit can!' she said indignantly as Steve made notes.

'What time did you get home that day?'

'Around six.'

'Anyone to vouch for that time?'

'Yes my husband, who as you know is not at home at the moment,' Emily said irritated at the questions.

'Do you know where your husband might be Mrs Lewis?' Moni asked.

'I think he is with his friend Mark, they like to have a boys' time together, whiskey and all that,' then in a slightly patronising tone said, 'Sara's widower…or rather her ex-husband.'

Steve gave a cursory glance at Moni which Emily spotted. She felt herself swallow, even though her mouth was dry, her heart lurched an extra beat, she felt dread. 'Do you suspect my husband?'

'Every piece of information has to be followed up, however small it is,' said Steve.

'Ok Mrs Lewis, we'll visit him at Mr Eaton's place.' Moni said.

'Oh he won't like that…'

'I will remind you again Mrs Lewis this is a murder enquiry and we may well have to ask you both to come down to the station for further questioning, purely voluntarily of course.'

'What now…?'

'We'll let you know when, possibly later this evening.'

Emily saw the detectives out and as she shut the door she felt a rush of anger at David. She picked up her mobile and phoned his number, but it went straight to voice mail, 'Please leave a message and I'll get back,' it said in his clear voice. She left a message then phoned Mark.

'Mark, I need to speak to David, now!' Emily said.

'Sorry Em, David's a little worse for wear at the moment I'll get him to phone you back as soon as poss,' my dear girl.'

'You're lying Mark, he's never that bad!'

Mark had a feeling this would backfire on him, he felt deceitful and wondered why he should cover up for that dick head of a husband. Their friendship was at an end, there was no need for loyalty. Mark thought too highly of Em, so sexy, so clever.

'Well we had a quarrel Em and he managed to cut his eye, bruising and all that stuff. To be truthful he's not here.'

'Then where the hell is he?'

'Probably at a Premier Inn for a couple of days, there's one in Horsham he's been to before.'

'Why should he use a Premier Inn in Horsham?'

'When he works late at the solicitors and has to finish some documentation for a client…'

'Yes I know he's done that before when he was working…, Emily remembered, 'Look Mark if the police should come round to you please tell them what you told me.'

'Oh God Em, he has a black eye you know!'

'Good,' she smiled to herself. 'Why did you hit him Mark?'

'We had a disagreement, you can sort this out with him when you see him. Now just leave me out of it Em, there's a good girl. I'd do anything for you, you know but sometimes it's complicated.'

Emily pressed end on her phone, then wrapped and hugged her coat around herself as she returned to the kitchen then poured another glass of wine and reset her microwave for a couple of minutes hoping her meal wouldn't be too chewy.

27

The steam from the cooking disappeared as it was sucked up into the extractor fan, it seemed, in a straight line. It was a noisy process that Harry could do without but he knew that as soon as the vegetables were cooked he could switch it off. It was Julie's idea to get one and although it was a pain, he knew she was right. There was nothing worse that filling the house with cooking smells, she would say. He prodded the carrots in the steamer, yes al dente just right he thought. The big moment came to shut the noise down and when he did he found his ears ringing for a few moments.

As he placed the carrots into the heating dish, Gina their neighbour, opened the kitchen door and with a sheepish smile looked around checking Harry was on his own.

'Ciao Harry,'

'Ah Gina,' Harry said pleased to see her, 'are you free for a few moments? I do need some help with dinner.' He showed her the bandaged hand, 'it's just that my hand is painful, I need to keep it elevated.

'Of course I can. I said I would help you anytime, you only need to let me know,' she said looking through her eye lashes at him. Harry knew she was flirting and smiled at her. He could handle her ok, as long as I get some help, he thought.

'There are four hungry guests sitting in the dining room, would you mind if I leave you in the kitchen whilst I offer them wine?'

'Of course I can, a glass of wine for me too I hope,' she said seductively in her native Italian accent.

*

It annoyed Julie that there were no parking spaces in Queen Street. Worthing was becoming like Brighton, where too many cars vie for space. She liked this town though, it was friendly and traffic wardens were more sympathetic. She knew this because there were less reports of assaults on them. There was a space just at the end of the road which meant she would walk about two hundred metres to Louise Brooks' house. The post code showed no numbe,r only a name - Tudor, and even though the sunset was bright against an icy blue sky, the ground was darker. She just hoped the house would be visibly lit and wished she'd taken Steve with her this time.

Louise answered the door and recognised Julie from the murder investigation team at the hospital and invited Julie in. Julie could see that Louise was nervous and decided to keep the interview as brief as possible.

'As you well know this is a murder enquiry...' Julie said.

'It's so dreadful I'm still coming to terms with Sara's death.' Louise said fidgeting with her fingers.

'You were friends with Sara?'

'No only colleagues.'

'Did you like Sara?'

Louise hesitated then said, 'No.'

Julie continued to ask about Sara's friendships, of any kind and noticed Louise was uncomfortable with imparting information. She had to remind her several times that this was a murder enquiry.

'Okay, well Sara was too friendly with the men. She had an affair with one of the anaesthetists and one of our managers...' Louise hesitated before she gave Julie their names, 'also Consultant Anaesthetist Dr Muller was really upset that Sara had been to his house and stirred up trouble with his wife…apparently Sara had thrown acid stuff on his car's paintwork…you can imagine he was furious. .' Julie sat quietly as Louise talked freely. '…and our manager was her next victim, God knows how many men she destroyed. She was obsessed with detail just like someone who had OCD. I hated going to work sometimes, it used to be so nice working with the lovely staff, and we all got on like a family. It all changed when *she* arrived, you know, Sara.' Louise blew out her cheeks and went on to say, 'My friend Daniel also got caught in her web too then tried to end it. He was hoping to get back with his long term girlfriend…actually he was discharged from the army suffering with post-traumatic stress disorder.' Louise sat back after blurting out all the information.

'Is he a violent man?'

'No but is apt to outbursts if cornered… more like a panic attack although they're less frequent these days.'

'And what's the manager's name?

'Alan Clarke deputy manager actually, but he's off at the moment. His wife died tragically in a flood about two, three weeks ago. I'm acting up in his absence.' Louise gave a smug smile.

Julie had temporarily forgotten this name, Will Partis had mentioned it the same day Harry was in accident and emergency, and because of the distraction she hadn't taken in his report. She would need to catch up with his report of that day as soon as she got back to the office. Julie stood to leave, and Louise accompanied her to the front door.

'What's Emily Lewis like as a boss? Julie asked.

'She's good at her job, very conscientious but she has been stressed with her husband recently, something to do with Sara, I dare say.'

'Why do you suppose this?'

'Well, Emily, had found a piece of paper with numbers on, meant nothing to her but her husband went into a rage when she showed it to him.'

'Why had this got something to do with Sara?'

'Um...well I just thought it may have been. Women's intuition?

Julie frowned at this remark then stopped in the hall and excused herself for needing to send a text to a colleague. She quickly instructed Moni to ask Emily Lewis about these numbers especially as she had sent Moni and Steve to the Lewis' place for more questioning.

'Oh… and Daniel, he's a family friend, he thought I'd sent him the numbers from my mobile phone, which I didn't but I forgot to put the passcode on and went to a meeting leaving it on Emily's desk. I can't help but feel Sara had used my phone…' Louise said rapidly.

'Why would Sara do that?' Julie asked.

'That's just the sort of thing I wouldn't put past Sara!' Louise smiled slightly maliciously.

'Would you know where Sara kept her own phone?'

'It might be in one of the old -lockers I've seen her using one of them but can't remember which one now. Most of them had to be broken into by works as staff kept forgetting their combination,' Louise said, 'if there's one that hasn't got a broken lock you could try that?'

'One last question, where were you on the night of twenty ninth November?'

'At home with my mum, she will vouch for me as I got in about seven that evening. We ate dinner not long after.'

'Thank you Louise is your mother in at the moment?'

'Yes would you like her to confirm this?' She called out to her mother who immediately corroborated the information. Julie was satisfied then left the Brooks' house. Her phone pinged a text - it was Steve they had just arrived at the Lewis's place and it was in darkness. She texted back for them to wait until someone arrived or try again later. This could be a long evening she said to herself.

After the recent finger slicing episode she texted Harry with a quick update on ETD. He promptly texted back, "Not to worry, Gina helping me out, we'll plate up a meal for you and leave it in the fridge. " finishing the text with a smiley face and kisses. Julie was not happy.

28

The wide driveway narrowed dramatically into a single lane which led to Mark Eaton's house. As Moni drove slowly Steve could see the house lights sparkle through the trees and they reminded him of a glitter ball.

She parked the shabby unmarked police car near to the house and smiled to herself at how incongruous it looked. They both got out of the car and stood back surveying the huge old building that had its lights on down stairs. It reminded her of a Dickensian Christmas scene.

'Steve you can take the lead and ask the questions.' She watched him straighten his jacket and give her a small quick smile, 'It'll be a good learning experience for you.' Steve nodded approval at her decision. This was what he wanted to fit in and be part of a team.

They approached the giant oak front door with black metal studs within each panel and the only means of alerting the occupant of their arrival was to pull a long metal rod with a stirrup type handle. It reminded Steve of the old style toilet cistern. He gripped the handle and gave a tug.

The door slowly opened and a slightly overweight man stood looking out at them. Steve introduced them.

'Good evening sir, my name is Detective Constable Hayes and this is my colleague Detective Sergeant Reece. We would like to speak to a Mr Mark Eaton please.' Both detectives showed their identity cards. The man scrutinized the proffered ID cards then looked up and said.

'Well I'm Mark Eaton... what can I do for you?'

'Sir we are trying to locate David Lewis and believe he is here?'

'He was earlier but left and I assumed he went home to his wife?'

'We've spoken to his wife who has not seen him for twenty four hours...would you know of his whereabouts?'

Mark gave a deep long sigh giving Steve a blast of his whisky breath which for a moment made Steve flinch - he hoped no one had noticed this.

'Quite possibly he's in a Premier Inn in Horsham near the railway station, he often uses this inn especially if he has a case to complete. It's near the law courts,' Mark said, 'he claims on expenses.'

Steve was quick to pick up on this and said. 'David Eaton still works?'

'Well…I have a feeling you are aware of his recent redundancy?

'Then why would he be at the inn sir?'

'As far as I'm aware he'd had a few words with his wife and decided to stay away for a few days or so. Quite ridiculous.'

As both the detectives turned to go, Moni asked, 'Do you get on well with David Lewis?'

'Well sometimes he annoys me - especially the way he treats his wife.'

'I understand he acted for you in your divorce?'

'That was weeks ago and I can't see what this has got to do with where he is now!'

'As you know Mr Eaton we are investigating your ex-wife's murder and sometimes we have to ask sensitive questions.'

'We may need to return at some stage Mr Eaton, if we have any more queries,' Steve added.

Moni heard the heavy door shut behind them and as soon as they reached their car Steve spoke his thoughts. 'He's hiding something, I know he is. He seems reluctant to give information, I mean, he appeared evasive and contradictory,' Steve said. 'One minute Mark Eaton says he thought David Lewis had returned home then the next he admits he knew the couple had had a row and that David was lying low for a few days…'

'Let's go find David Lewis and see what he has to say, eh?' Moni said.

The Premier Inn laid was back off the road, it was easy to find and the reception staff were helpful. They contacted David Lewis's room number and announced that two detectives needed to speak to him. Instead of inviting them to his room he arranged to meet them in the foyer, by the reception. Moni said it was not private enough and the reluctant David agreed to use his room. Steve wondered if there was a woman involved somewhere. Moni hoped they could conduct the interview without interruptions.

'Mr Lewis why have you come to the Premier inn?' asked Moni.

'Because I need to get my thoughts together!' David hissed back.

'You sound upset, what has caused this?'

'Well that's none of your business…'

'It is our business, as you know we are investigating the murder of your friend's ex-wife.'

'Oh God, look I had words with my wife and I thought a few days apart would help settle things down.'

'What words, sir, can you elaborate?' Steve said.

'Well it was over something silly really.'

'Please tell us.'

'She, my wife, found some numbers which mean absolutely nothing to me. She was going on about it like a dog with a bone, she would not let go. Of course this caused us to have words.'

Moni read the numbers and message to him, *'Fourteen, phone you at the usual time, take good care of our secret phone.'* She looked up at David and noticed his lips were dry and he made a few small choking gasps. 'I take that as a yes that you do know about this and who sent it to you?'

'Yes I am familiar with this silly message, means nothing to me, I assure you.'

'Your wife said you had a mystery phone and that you denied it was yours, perhaps from a secret lover?'

'This is ridiculous...' David became irritated.

Steve added, 'How did you get that black eye sir?' David looked away and sat down hard on his bed and put his head in his hands.

He suddenly looked up with an anxious expression then he said, 'Look I was having an affair which was just a fling type one, you know.' He looked at Steve for a man to man understanding. Moni was curious as to how Steve would react, and kept quiet.

'Who were you having an affair with sir?' Steve asked.

'That doesn't matter, it was an affair that lasted...oh maybe a few weeks on and off, she wanted to return my personal items to my wife!'

'Did she return them?' Steve asked.

'Yes she did but to me thank God! Emily doesn't know about any of this and I'd appreciate it staying that way, too.'

'Was this affair with Sara Eaton, your friend's ex-wife?'

David stood, then approached Steve menacingly but Steve stood his ground and waited for an answer. 'It's just that, sir, we cannot assume, we need confirmation and evidence. This is a serious crime, murder sir.'

'Yes it was Sara Eaton.' David growled. 'I got my black eye from a disagreement with her ex-husband.' There was a moments silence before Moni spoke.

'We'll need you to accompany us down to the station for more questioning and I suggest you book out of this inn now,' Moni added, feeling proud that Steve had remembered not to assume anything. Yes he did well today, she thought.

29

The atmosphere within the kitchen was changing by the second and Julie felt a show-down would erupt any moment. Even Harry was banging the saucepans about which only went to fuel the tension and she didn't want a row. She was tired with trying to juggle home with work and now there was the neighbour's involvement, or was this a figment of her imagination? Julie's guilt increased. Harry turned to her and said, 'Look Julie, let's not start to quarrel, we've always talked things through, haven't we?'

She took a deep breath and felt tears prick her eyes as she turned to face him. 'I know Harry it's ridiculous isn't it?' And gave a wan smile.

'It's all to do with Gina isn't it?' he said and took Julie's hands into his good hand, 'there's absolutely nothing going on apart from me needing a little help in the kitchen.' He brought up his bandaged hand and waggled it in front of her. 'Look darling we need to get away let's get your sister over, she loves all this work?'

'Good idea Harry, except I do have a murder to solve first,' she grimaced, 'then I'll put in for leave, how's that for a plan?'

Harry nodded his approval and said. 'I'll still need help with chores so what do you suggest?'

'Use Gina on the strict proviso that you pay her from the petty cash!' Julie said in mock chide.

The back door opened and a cheery Gina stepped into the kitchen, she flicked her dark bob style hair. 'Ciao Harry!' Gina called out in her soft sexy voice, then in a panic realising he wasn't there broke out into a loud and friendly tone. She gave Julie a nervous smile.

'Ciao Gina,' Julie said, 'Harry is serving drinks to the guests.'

'He usually brings a glass out for me too,' she said fluttering her dark Italian eyes, only to impress another woman. To Julie, Gina looked like an over decorated Christmas tree dripping with gold dangly ear rings, medallions swung from her neck and bangles jangled on each movement.

'Harry and I have decided to pay you for your help so far,' Julie felt good to be in control, 'probably for another couple of weeks until his stitches are removed?'

'Prego.' Gina said coldly. As she left the kitchen a sickly scent lingered in the air from cheap perfume that had been sprayed on heavily. It left a horrible taste in Julie's mouth.

*

Julie returned to the incident room back at the police station, she intended to update the board since she had another suspect to add. It seemed puzzling with the latest revelation of strange numbers that Louise Brooks had a possible phone hack. Moni and Steve arrived into the office. 'We have David Lewis in the interview room, ma'am.' Steve said.

'Why?' Julie asked.

'His account of his actions and whereabouts have been contradictory and he seems reluctant to elaborate. Basically I feel he is hiding more than his wife knows,' said Steve.

Julie looked at Moni who just raised her eyebrows and shrugged her shoulders as if to say, Steve made this decision. Julie gave a slight nod and said, 'as long as you haven't arrested him, we do need evidence this time. Do you feel he is a person of interest?'

'Most definitely ma'am,' said the eager to please Steve

'Good, we don't want to upset our Chief Super!' Julie said. 'So what do you have on David Lewis?'

Steve filled her in with the details so far while Moni added about the numbers. Julie who was looking at the board wondering where to put David Lewis's photo, turned to Moni with an incredulous look as if someone had made a bad smell and didn't want to own up to it. 'Numbers…that's strange, Louise Brooks had numbers on her phone which were meant for Daniel Franks- another possible person of interest, and she reckons that someone had used her phone or hacked it.' The adrenaline started to kick in, Julie felt something was not adding up. Her heart thumped away perhaps a little too much.

'Doesn't she use a passcode on her phone?' asked Steve.

'Sadly not all the time…' said Julie, 'no way of telling who used it, perhaps Sara Eaton prior to her death. Seems she got up to a lot of mischief with phones.'

There was anticipation in the office as the detectives sat pondering the board. No one spoke for some minutes- it was reminiscent of exam conditions where full concentration was needed. Every so often tongues would click and then the occasional short intake of breath as if someone was about to speak but decided not to. Julie went to the board took a look at the numbers then said.

'Could these numbers be connected in some way like a code?'

'Sara Eaton was mixed race Chinese, I wonder if it means something in that culture?' said Steve.

'Her aunt in Folkestone…what did the local CID find out about her?' asked Moni.

'Good point, Moni. I don't think they asked the right questions perhaps Steve and I will go to Folkestone tomorrow…' Julie sat down heavily on the main desk as if trying to stop it from moving away.

Steve looked relieved that he'd been chosen to accompany the boss. 'I'll make notes of questions ma'am, especially about the Chinese culture.'

'In the meantime we need to question David Lewis.' said Moni.

David Lewis sat anxiously at a lone table in a sparse room with high dirty windows that obviously took the brunt of the weather. He was bored with his wait until a uniformed officer entered carrying a tray of coffee and cake. He placed it in front of David who thanked him. The officer told him that soon the detectives would be in to speak to him, David looked over to the two way glass mirror wondering if they were sitting supping a drink and watching him. Clearly hoping to unsettle him with the long wait.

The cake was out of date by a month but he'd not eaten for a few hours and decided to give it a go. It was more like bread pudding but all the same he ate and swished it down with his lovely hot coffee. He did feel more human afterwards.

As if on cue the door of the interview room opened again and in walked two detectives DS Reece and DC Hayes. They were polite but then David thought it a ploy to help relax him further. For God's sake it's been a good hour that I've been left to stew, you morons he thought then he gave his most friendly smile as if to be pleased to see the two detectives.

They sat down opposite David, switched on the digital deck recorder and proceeded to inform David that he had not been arrested as he had come to the station voluntarily to help with enquiries into the murder of Sara Eaton. Steve Hayes read out David's name and details as is customary and the interview started.

'Why did you have a spare phone? asked Steve, 'your wife Emily said she had found it in your sports bag?'

'In answer to your question DC Hayes, first it's not my spare phone and secondly I thought it was left by a friend.'

'And it was in your sports bag? Steve asked sternly, almost sarcastically. 'What is your friend's name?'

'In answer to your first question DC Hayes, quite possibly someone thought it was their bag… it probably belonged to my friend,' he said shifting in his seat.

'And your friend's name?'

'Um…Mark Eaton,' David answered back sarcastically.

'The deceased's ex-husband?'

'Yes.'

'And was it his?'

'No.'

'Let's make it easier for all of us, you say who the phone belongs to and we'll be able to check?' Moni Reece said, slightly patronisingly.

'Okay, it was Sara Eaton's phone, she gave it to me, it was part of our...um, a means of meeting up, occasionally.' David couldn't believe he was owning up to this bloody phone business.

'How long had you and Sara been, meeting-up?'

'Too long - she became a liability!' David said caustically. 'Well it was more on odd occasions really,' he added dismissively.

Both detectives sat patiently waiting for David to add more, but instead he looked down at his hands and as they fidgeted, realising how that may look, he scooped both hands into his lap and continued to fidget out of sight.

'Did you kill Sara Eaton, David?' asked Moni.

'No I bloody well didn't! Although I could name a few who'd like to...she deserved what she got, she was a bitch. She caused the fire in my kitchen, she threatened to bring my toiletries back when Emily was at home! There were so many other wicked things she did... ' He stopped himself he'd already said too much. He felt his mouth go dry and knew the detectives had noticed it too.

'We'd like the names of those few,' said Steve

'Alan Clark for one, his wife lost her life due to a row about her so called friend Sara, who had an affair with him!

'Thank you David. And who else?' David hesitated as he rolled his eyes.

'Well Owen Muller a doctor at the hospital, Sara broke up his marriage and possibly the surgical rep...Daniel? Yes she fucked up his chances of getting together with his ex...see what I mean? So many hated her and of course her ex-husband. He hated her with a vengeance, I should know I was his solicitor in the divorce case.' David now felt like an informant, a slanderer. He'd dealt with too many clients in the past that loved to gossip. The two detectives appeared unfazed by his admission and thanked him for his help. David thought his ordeal was over, he was amazed at the officer's tactics. He licked his lips as Steve asked if he wanted another coffee break. David nodded yes, a little more subdued.

'Who gave you this information Mr Lewis?' asked Moni when Steve left to get coffee.

'Well my wife and her acting manager Louise Brooks, who seems to know a lot.' Moni made notes for herself to speak to them later.'I wonder if I could use the loo in a moment?' David said. He appeared shaky as he stood to leave the interview room. As he entered the men's toilet a smell of strong stale urine caught him by surprise, like a monkey house at a zoo where the apes would pee indiscriminately. He heaved at its aroma. The urinals were disgusting with soggy paper that sabotaged its own draining, the usual pubic hair floated on its stagnant surface. He heaved again.

Back in the interview David felt a little more refreshed. He thought how clever the questioning was and how ridiculous he had been to say so much. But too late, he sat down and the interview commenced. This time he would not be so free and easy with information and decided to limit his intelligence, he'd said too much already.

'Let me take you back to the day of your kitchen fire, did you order a Chinese take-away from Henfield?' asked Moni.

'No but Emily stopped on the way home and ordered one, she felt sorry for me because of the fire…'

'Apparently another take-away from the same place was delivered to you a little while later, who was that from?'

'That I didn't know at the time until Sara asked if I liked the meal, she had the Chinese takeaway delivered then I knew.'

'Why did she come up to Henfield from Worthing and pay cash for it?'

'God knows, maybe she wanted to intimidate me further.'

'Why further?'

'She phoned me from Emily's mobile phone, I thought it was Emily until Sara spoke. I was furious especially as she said she'd sprayed Emily's perfume on herself, we had a row. I was so incensed with the fact she had been in Emily's office drawer. That was when I smelt burning from my kitchen and the sound of our fire alarm. The place would have gone up in smoke if I hadn't acted quickly, fire brigade and all that.'

'So we take it that you were having quite an affair with her?'

'Not a big one just an occasional…meet up, nothing much really.'

'Your wife was not aware?' asked Moni coldly.

'As I've said before, it just happened and there is no need for my wife to ever know.'

'She will find out at some stage Mr Lewis and it would be a good idea to inform her now rather than later.'

'Yes… in my own good time,' he growled at Moni, clearly feeling trapped.

The two officers sat quietly, it reminded David of a panel of judges, deliberating.

30

All she wanted at this moment was normality, whatever that was but clearly with the latest developments, none of this would be on the agenda. As Louise paused to reflect, Emily walked in and gave her a serious stare, she looked stressed about something, probably David giving her grief again. As if reading Louise's mind Emily said that David had been taken to the police station for questioning as several other men had been interviewed too, helping the police with their enquiries.

'Oh God, who's been interviewed so far?' Louise asked not quite knowing what else to say. She did think of Daniel and wondered if he'd been taken in after all he had a motive.

'I'm not sure exactly but David and Owen have been of interest.'

'Most definitely Owen….'Louise trailed off turning her head with a half-smile.

'Why?'

'Sara had thrown acid over his car last month and threatened to tell his wife of their affair,' Louise gave a sheepish smile, 'all he wanted was revenge.'

'How come I wasn't aware of this?'

'I hate getting involved with work stuff, it's going on all the time,' Louise leant forward as if to confide, then thought differently of it. Emily waited for her to compose herself then said,

'Do the police know about this?'

'Possibly…'

'Is there anything about David you need to tell me, Louise?'

'Daniel, is a family friend, the surgical rep from last month, he said he saw Sara with an unknown man then the next day with Owen. He thought they were just colleagues so didn't ask her about them as he already had a date with her,' Louise said. 'It seems she was stringing all of them along…. did you know we called her The Fatal Attraction?'

31

Rachael Crosby told her husband Jim to contact the police now that they were back home. At first he was reluctant but as she stood over him quite menacingly he did as he was told, after all she was almost paranoid in Florida that the US police were looking out for them.

'Shoreham Police,' said a dour voice.

'I need to speak to someone about a suspicious death in the hospital where I'm housekeeping. I think I may have some important information,' his heart skipped a beat and he felt his voice go weak with the realisation of what he was about to say. Withholding evidence or whatever it's called he thought, was a criminal offence, he thought. He gulped then had this sudden urge to slam the phone down but as he said he was a housekeeper there, they would soon put two and two together. Rachael eyeballed him.

'Hold on sir and I'll put you through to one of the MCT officers.'

Within seconds a woman answered. 'Hello sir, I'm one of the MCT investigating officers on the case of the recent death at a hospital and I understand you have some information regarding this recent murder…but first if I could just take your details.' said the officer. Murder, murder, oh my God its murder, he thought in a panic as Rachael watched his face. He felt a wave of panic, then nausea as bile rose in his throat. Will they accuse him of this crime, how could he prove it wasn't him? He suddenly felt faint as he held the phone tight. A voice suddenly spoke bringing him back to his senses.

'Hello Mr Crosby. I'm DC Steve Hayes, you may remember me interviewing you at Southlands Hospital. You've been away to Florida with your family, I understand?'

Jim hesitated then stammered. 'Yes… got back last…um, last night and thought I'd… um better contact you.' Jim paused, wondering how to admit to his minor theft. As he sat pondering his mouth dry was enough for his tongue to stick to the roof of his mouth. He felt guilt and fear by his own actions. It reminded him of when he was a young boy and had to admit to mischief, but then it was mostly the fear of punishment being dished out which is what he felt now….

'Would you like me to visit you Mr Crosby?' Without a moment's hesitation Jim blurted a yes.

Steve went on his own as he'd already taken a statement on the night of Sara Eaton's death and wondered if Jim Crosby was aware it was now a murder enquiry as he had been away for the week.

As Steve approached the Crosby's house he spotted Jim looking out the window. Steve parked nearby and when he got to their door it was already open. Jim greeted him and showed him into the living room.

'What is it you want to add Mr Crosby?' Steve asked.

'I found a broken smart phone and didn't think straight I was tired and needed this holiday. I didn't want to get off late as our flight was early and….'

'Okay just tell me about the phone, was it from the crime scene and do you still have it Sir?'

'Yes… it's still in my work bag where I put it that night.' Hearing this was a relief to Steve as he took out his latex gloves and evidence bag for forensics.

'Will I get into trouble for keeping it?'

'It's an obstruction to our enquiry to keep crucial evidence for such a serious crime, especially as this is a murder investigation.'

'Oh my God, will I be arrested…could I lose my job?'

'I will speak to my senior officer, it is a serious matter removing items from the scene of a crime but I will let you know,' said Steve. 'The fact that you have admitted it and contacted us goes in your favour.'

The MCT and Julie were piecing together and updating the incident board.'We have three persons of interest at the moment and when Will, gets back hopefully, with more info on Alan Clarke, he could be the third person of interest.' Julie paused for thought. 'Dr Muller has no alibi, David Lewis has an alibi - he was at home with his wife who has vouched for him. We need to get an alibi from Daniel Franks. Steve and I will visit him later this morning.' She paused again. 'But first Steve, you can find out from Jim Crosby if he heard any strange goings on between eight and ten the estimated time of Ms Eaton's death.'

*

Jim Crosby sat quietly hoping the police would be lenient with him for keeping such crucial evidence. He didn't think at the time it would be a problem but now he felt stupid. He kept shaking his head in disbelief at his actions and relief that he'd given the phone to the police. Bloody hell, it could mean prison and losing his job, he thought.

Jim kept fidgeting with his hands, an irritating habit he had when he was anxious. He looked at Steve in anticipation.

'What else can I say?' Jim asked now wringing the life out of his fingers.

'Well I'm going to ask some questions Jim, about anything else you may have missed on the night of the murder.'

'Oh my God, the murder, it sounds awful…' Jim looked tearful.

'I want you to think back on that night, was there anything else strange that happened?' Steve asked. Jim put his index finger to his mouth, clearly in thought. Steve sat patiently then Jim said,

'I left the female changing room to see about the alarm going off and when I got back there was a pair of theatre clogs on the floor, looked like someone had just kicked them off.'

'Could you have knocked them down from somewhere…?'

'Nah, they were kicked off alright, they had initials on the heels like the rest…'

'Initials?'

'Yeah, not sure what they were,' Jim sat back and looked up to the ceiling, deep in thought then said emphatically, 'EB.'

'Anything else?'

'No just EB.'

'No I meant anything else out of the ordinary?'

'Yes a couple of times I caught a glimpse of someone leaving the theatre unit strange, I didn't actually see any one just their shadow, looked like a tall man with dark hair.'

'What time was this?'

'Well, um…first time around eight then the next time about eight thirty ish.'

Steve wrote this in the new statement then asked Jim to sign it. 'If you think of anything else Jim, please write it down and contact me, anytime.' Steve handed him a card with two extension numbers under the police logo. As Jim took it he thought how thin the card felt, more like thick paper. He wondered if this was something to do with cutting costs much like the NHS, every little helps.

32

Much to Steve's relief Julie volunteered to take her car, a nice change from the smelly police pool cars which left him feeling dirty and stank of unidentifiable aromas. The fact that the seats were always stained with dubious marks that never saw a steam clean would be something for forensic interest.

Finding Daniel Franks' place was easy for a change. Only four terraced houses clearly marked with numbers, one to four, Short Row, Daniel Franks was number one. Julie parked her car nearby and they walked the fifty yards to Daniel Franks' door and rang his bell. They waited a reasonable length of time then rang it again followed by a knock. Steve had been caught out many times before with defunct bells. He wondered why people bothered with bells at all as most of the time they were taped over. As there was still no answer they could reasonably presume that he was out.

'No one in... we'll come back later, Steve.' The two detectives turned to go when a car pulled up into the small parking area in front of number one. A tall dark haired man got out staring quizzically at them.

Steve spoke first, 'Hello sir we are looking for Daniel Franks.'

'Look no further, what can I do for you?' Daniel said politely.

Both detectives showed their ID when Julie said, 'We are investigating the murder of Sara Eaton.'

'Oh…. ,'Daniel narrowed his eyes, 'then you'd better come on it then,' he said, as he opened his front door.

The first impression of the interior was typical ex-army, tidy and orderly. There was a strong aroma of what seemed to be WD40 which hung in the air. Daniel noticed the way Julie screwed up her nose. Daniel smiled at that, then explained. 'I'm a surgical rep, mostly for operating theatres and I've just finished two months at Southlands Hospital demonstrating different instruments and it's down me to keep equipment maintained, well oiled.'

'I'll get straight to the point Mr Franks, we are investigating the murder of Sara Eaton who we believe you were having an affair with,' 'stated Julie.

'Oh...um yes but our affair only lasted for about a couple of weeks or so...I called it a day as I was trying to rekindle a past relationship.'

'How did Sara take that?' asked Steve.

Daniel lowered his gaze for a few seconds as if he had something to hide. Both detectives noticed this change in demeanour and left him to answer in his own time. 'I told Sara over the phone that I didn't want to continue with the relationship, she seemed okay about it,' he paused then shrugged his shoulders, 'except later that same evening, I was sitting in the pub waiting for my girlfriend... I'd booked a table at the Red Lion pub earlier, when Sara arrived, how she knew I was there beats me. She acted strangely as she plonked this huge plastic bag on my table, thank God my date hadn't arrived at that moment.' Daniel sat quietly for a moment his whole manner less composed as he wrung his hands clearly becoming agitated at recounting the experience.

'What was in the bag?' Julie asked softly, not wanting to trigger emotion of any kind.

'A mixture of men's wash stuff, you know deodorants, aftershave, shaving foam...not all the stuff belonged to me, in fact only a toothbrush, that was all I had owned in that bag,' he said, seething at the thought. 'I couldn't believe it when she turned up, I didn't tell her about my date...' His voice trailed off as he put his head in his hands.

'What was your reaction to this, Daniel?' Steve asked.

'I just lost the plot, upended the table, smashing my half full beer glass onto the floor!' He paused to reflect on this. 'She just stood there indifferent. Bitch.' He paused again. 'Then the bar staff shouted at me, one called the police and a crowd of lads came running round from another part of the bar, apparently to protect the so - called lady!' Daniel started to rock slowly back and forth in his seat as he recalled the incident, 'I still suffer post-traumatic stress from the army, I was stationed in Afghanistan...I have learnt a technique to calm myself but this...just did me in that night.'

'What happened next?' Julie asked, not wanting to get involved with delicate issues to do with any form of mental illness, as she felt unequipped to deal with anything beyond her scope of investigation and hoped she showed enough sensitivity.

'The police arrived and arrested me or whatever it's called, so that I would calm down. Basically they took me away at the moment my date arrived…badly timed…I knew I'd blown any chance of reconciliation, end of.'

Julie felt she was losing him now and suggested a cup of something to help him compose himself. Steve offered to make tea. Daniel rubbed his face hard and ran his hand through his dark hair. He seemed relieved that there was a break. He leant back in his seat and looked up at the ceiling, appearing restless. He didn't look Julie in the eye when she asked, 'Where were you on the night of twenty ninth November Daniel?'

'Um…well I was here most of the evening then had to pop out to collect some equipment.' He gave a deep sigh and remained quiet. Julie felt he was hiding something, he still didn't look her in the eye. She didn't have a hunch but she knew he was hiding something.

'Where did you go?'

'Oh…well, um…,' his eyes darted back and forth as if looking for an answer, then he gave a wry smile as he looked Julie in the eye, 'I went to the hospital… to collect the last of my equipment. I needed to sort it out ready for Monday.' He grimaced a smirk which Julie thought was more of an apology.

'Couldn't it have waited 'til then?' Julie said.

'Well I suppose so but I just wanted to get everything packed away…,' he hesitated, then looked at Julie and said, 'one of the staff was still there, an anaesthetist I think, yet he was wearing a sweat shirt over jeans he was busy in the anaesthetic room maybe putting things away. Unfortunately that was where I'd left this particular show case. He was quite put out with me actually being there but I didn't need to stay long just got the case…still got to collect another but thought I'd pop back later maybe Monday.'

'What time was this?'

'Around early evening, between nineteen and twenty hundred hours, perhaps. I thought the theatre would be empty by then…I think I surprised him when I turned up.' Then he added, 'thought I saw another staff member leave from somewhere…didn't take much notice as we didn't speak.'

'So you went to the hospital that evening, an anaesthetist was upset that you were there?' Julie frowned, 'Can you describe the 'anaesthetist'?'

'Not as tall as me six three maybe. He had dark scruffy hair, slim, creased up blue jeans and grey sweat shirt.'

'Then you saw another staff leave, male or female?'

'I'm not sure if that staff was leaving or arriving but was shortish in statue. I knew the housekeeper would be up there at that time and wanted to avoid him, as I shouldn't have been in the hospital at all. I'm not staff...you know...didn't want to be stopped - I was in a hurry.' Daniel took a sip from his mug of tea, and licked his lips as he cupped his hot drink.

'In a hurry?'

'Look I know this looks bad but I had to be quick, didn't want to explain my presence in case he made a fuss. I sneaked in, got my case and tried to sneak out but he heard me go, and called after me, I ran off quickly down the stairs. No one saw me.'

'Any security?' Steve asked.

'Nah not there.'

Steve caught Julie's eye and he knew they'd have to take a statement at the station.'Daniel Franks we need you to accompany us to the police station for further questioning, you are not under arrest. You are helping us with our enquiries.' Julie said.

Daniel looked shocked at this development. 'I didn't kill her you know, I've not hurt anyone…. I just get panic attacks that's all.'

33

Chief Superintendent Defoe stood looking at the team with a quizzical expression then said, 'Where's DI Robertson?' It startled the officers who looked at each other for confirmation. Knowing Defoe was ambulating into their domain was a near trespass into unknown territory. 'Well as soon as you find her I need an update,' he said, addressing Moni who he knew was more senior in Julie's absence.

'Yes sir,' Moni said politely. Defoe articulated a grunt, turned and went back upstairs to his office leaving the staff smiling in relief as Moni phoned Julie.

*

Daniel sat down and looked around at the austere furnishing, it didn't really bother him - he'd been in worse places. There were areas of chipped off paint on the walls, the table had been fixed to the floor and the chairs in the room were clearly made of plastic to minimise any damage if the interviewee decided to throw a fit of frustration. Obviously Health and Safety had issued a precaution on selecting suitable furniture without making the room look too plain. Even the integral wall mirror would be smash proof so that even plastic furniture wouldn't penetrate it. The sickly airless smell reminded Daniel of a busy gym; sweaty and stuffy.

Daniel knew the mirror was two way and as he stared at it he couldn't help but notice a smear on his face, probably oil he thought, and smiled at himself as he wiped it off.

The two detectives entered the room and both sat down opposite Daniel. Steve led the questioning. Julie thought it would be good experience for him. They'd only been in the room for a couple of minutes when Julie's phone pinged a message, Steve started the interview process as Julie quickly checked her phone, it was Harry apologising for texting at work but as it was their nineteenth wedding anniversary, should he book a table at the Chardonnay along the A24? Rolling her eyes, she sighed. She had forgotten and knew that she couldn't plan anything anyway, she should've remembered. Now he'll be shitty to her later for putting work first. He knows what her job is like and this made her angry, so she sent a text back saying *"Let's eat at home tonight,"* hoping that would suffice. She made a note to google wedding anniversaries at least she would have the right gift…hopefully.

Meanwhile Steve carried on but kept glancing over to Julie anxious that she, his boss, paid attention. He felt it was less than professional and knew that Daniel had picked up on this by the way he frowned at Julie then him.

Daniel had already told them of his visit to the hospital the evening that Sara had been murdered, in fact there were two visits that night. He knew he would have to mention this.

'Okay Daniel, we'll record this interview for this case's benefit,' Steve said proudly, now feeling in control. 'On your visit back to Southlands Hospital on the night of the twenty ninth of November did you meet anyone that could corroborate your alibi?'

'Well yes but I don't know his name just that he was possibly an anaesthetist and didn't say much to me. He appeared irritated that I was looking through my show case.'

'What was in the case?' Steve asked.

'Surgical equipment as I have said already, I'm a rep and my job is to spend at least a month with a hospital, demonstrating latest techniques.'

'Why was the equipment still at the hospital?'

'Well I was going to leave it 'til Monday but decided to collect on Friday, lots to maintain.' Daniel said with a wave of his hand.

'Did anyone else see you at the hospital?'

'Um…sort of…apart from the anaesthetist and one of the staff, oh also I was heard again on the second time,' Steve looked at Julie.

'A second time?' asked Steve incredulously.

'Yes…,' Daniel looked cross with himself, pursed his lips then said, 'I knew the housekeeper would be up there and just wanted to avoid him. Especially the second time, I didn't want to bump into him as I shouldn't have been in the hospital at all. As I said earlier I'm not staff…you know…didn't want to be stopped, I was in a hurry,' he paused, looking up at the ceiling. 'As I said before, I had to be quick, didn't want to explain my presence in case he made a fuss. And the second time, I sneaked in around twenty thirty hours, got my last case then as I tried to sneak out he heard me and called after me, I ran off quickly down the stairs. No one else saw me, well maybe the other staff I told you about.'

'So it was the second visit you saw the other staff?' Steve asked. 'Was the 'anaesthetist' still there?

'The anaesthetist wasn't there and yes the other person, staff, looked like he or she was leaving but I don't really know.'

'You said there was no security at the hospital, no CCTV?' Julie asked.

'That's right, nothing… but I was worried he'd phone the police.'

Steve believed Daniel, then asked, 'Did you notice anything unusual while you were there, each time?' Daniel brought his hand up to his mouth tugging at his lips he looked ahead as if remembering and for a moment, he looked away deliberating almost as if he was looking for something to add. His eyes were darting around as if he was back in the theatre environment. Both detectives waited patiently.

'Yes. The fire door at the end of the clean corridor had been wedged open, that's where my last case had been kept in a cupboard nearby.' Daniel gave a puzzled frown. 'I thought perhaps the housekeeper had done it for some reason or another.'

Julie interrupted with a cough. 'We'll need the name of your company so we can verify you,' he added, as she gave a side glance at Steve who knew immediately he should have taken that information earlier and felt a little angry at himself for forgetting the most fundamental check.

It was Steve's job to find out who the 'anaesthetist' was that day and decided to visit the hospital to speak with manager Emily Lewis and get a list of staff who had access. Even though Daniel had managed to sneak in twice.

The manager was harassed when Steve arrived but she knew better than to keep him waiting. She passed him a newly printed list of staff and the possible anaesthetist that afternoon. She couldn't understand why the anaesthetist and one of the staff had been there at that time of evening. This intrigued Steve and he wondered if Daniel would recognise either person again.

In the meantime Moni contacted the Folkestone CID to get an update on the visit to Sara's Aunt Maggie. She felt they could have asked a few more questions or followed some through. She decided to visit the aunt herself but would wait for Steve to return from the hospital first.

*

Chief Superintendent Defoe sat patiently as Julie proudly reeled off the persons of interest like a compendium. He seemed pleased but when he jutted his chin and steepled his fingers Julie knew the signs as he expressed the need for evidence. 'We need to instil public confidence in the police, Julie.' She tried to sound upbeat but his chin remained jutted as he stared at her. He seemed pleased that the leads were coming together and yet irritated that the group of suspects was growing by the minute.

His desk was meticulously tidy, with an ornamental frame that held a photo of his wife and daughter with their pet spaniel. Every so often he adjusted - it probably as part of his compulsive disorder, then he picked something off the sleeve of his jacket and flicked it onto the floor. He gave a small smile and congratulated her on the team's work so far which Julie felt was more patronising than praising, then he reminded her the murder was a week old. Julie took a look out of the window and Defoe followed her gaze with a frown.

'Is there a problem Julie?'

'No sir, just a little tired today as we are working flat out and 'til late in the evening.'

'Well that's policing, our job Julie,' he said, still jutting his chin, his fingers now together up into a straight point as if he was praying, an annoying habit he had when he wanted to show his superiority. She smiled, stood and made her way to the door. As she was leaving he said, 'I have great faith in you Julie.'

As Julie got back to the office all heads swivelled around to her, trying to gauge her expression, the mood of Defoe. 'It's okay folks he only wanted an update so let's get on and try to get some evidence.' As she said that they realised Defoe had applied some pressure.

One of the civilian staff who spent most of her time researching new evidence turned to Julie and said. 'Steve just phoned in, said he has a list of staff from the theatre department but wanted Daniel Franks to identify that anaesthetist, they may need to get some photos of the staff.'

'So get on to it pronto. Phone Steve back and tell him to get photos...' Julie said, a little too abruptly. MCT staff noticed her change of mood and became extra busy just to please her. Julie went into her office. 'Where's Moni?' she called out.

'Here ma'am.' She stood and made her way to the office, 'I'm waiting for Steve's return so we can go down to Folkestone to re interview the aunt. I have a hunch that she knows more.'

'Good idea Moni,' Julie said with a smile, 'we need more hunches.' Julie liked it when Moni had gut feelings, invariably they lead on to the right tract. 'Get Will, to follow through the photo fit with Daniel so you can both get going when Steve arrives.'

Someone had put the espresso machine on and the coffee aroma wafted around, someone had left an open packet of custard creams near the mugs even so Moni checked her bag for chocolate biscuits wondering if she had enough to go round…. the mood in the office had become a little more upbeat and productive. Julie stayed in her office reading earlier actions that had been left on her desk. Most of these were predictable except for one, she studied it, stood and came back out to the incident board.

'I have something here…'she said, 'it seems Sara's mother's name was Suwen Li Crawford and she died in a private nursing home, Dale Lodge in Folkestone, twelve years ago.' Julie tapped her mouth with the action as she stared out the dirty window at a brick wall which was the back of the police cells. Everyone knew better than to speak at that moment. Julie was thinking. She looked at Moni. 'Crawford?'

'Sara's maiden name was Li then Eaton when she married.' Moni said.

'Okay…her mother was a Li, Chinese. Why did Sara keep her mother's Chinese name, had the mother remarried?'

'Um…. I've made a note to ask the aunt…'Moni said slowly as if she was trying to remember something she paused then said, 'Just thought, ma'am, there's an ITU doctor with the name of Crawford…. coincidence?'

'Was he checked out?'

'I'll check that this action was carried out, ma'am.' Moni said but Julie could already see the colour draining from Moni's face.

The office suddenly become a haven of activity with clicking key boards, phone calls with their undulating and sometimes hushed voices created a call centre atmosphere. Coffee mugs thudded the desk tops with biscuit packets that crisped under the pressure of each removal gaving a new credence, a new lease of life to the team. Julie returned to her office, dropped herself in to her chair but could not resist taking a look at Moni who was now on the phone, and it looked like she was talking on this phone to the civilian computer staff by the door and knew it was to have the doctor checked out. Why didn't Moni do this earlier? Julie felt the beginning of a rage, probably out of frustration. After all she was supposed to have a good team on this case and anything fundamental like a police check seemed too much to comprehend. Defoe had rightly spotted her stress but she was not going to buckle. Harry didn't help with his new kitchen friend…. Julie felt the stinging of tears just as Moni came into the office to confirm she was on the case. It was good that she had been honest with her mistake of not checking earlier. Moni noticed her boss's tears, but didn't mention anything.

'I'll take Steve to Folkestone and you can carry on with your action.' Julie said blowing her nose.

Steve and Will managed to pick up staff photos and took them to Daniel Franks to identify. He pointed to the photo of Alan Clark, even though he didn't see all of his face, he was fairly sure it was him.

'Bring him in,' said Julie, 'Will and Moni can interview him but I want to be aware of all details.' The tension in the office had now borne a fresh determination with a new suspect; not all bad, thought Julie.

34

Steve got out of the car leaving Julie to finish her phone call. He looked up at the detached 1940s house before him with its mock Tudor façade and noticed the front door was already open and there stood a handsome late- middle aged woman with perfectly coifed long white hair drawn back into a plait that hung down her back. Her Bohemian style of fashion suited her well and with so many bangles on her left arm Steve wondered how heavy they must be to lug around, as they looked to be expensive – made of silver and gold, yet the woman seemed unfazed by the jangling jewellery as she beamed a welcoming smile.

'Ms Denning?' Julie asked the smiling woman.

'Oh please call me Maggie,' the woman said directing the two detectives in to her house.

Both detectives showed their ID, and Maggie took a cursory look at them, 'Yes I know who you are,' another smile, 'go through to the living room and I'll get my housekeeper to make a tray of something.' Maggie disappeared off somewhere as Julie and Steve did as they were told.

They sat on one of the three sofas and looked around the room at the expensive décor, most of the furniture appeared Chinese in origin. There were many photos on the walls and surfaces, some looked like family groups and there was one on its own of Sara and presumably another one with her mother, clearly in happier times as both wore smiles. It was hard to tell who was who in some of the photos and as Maggie returned with the housekeeper trailing behind carrying a large tray, she spotted Julie studying the pictures.

'I'll tell you who's who in a moment,' she said acknowledging Julie's interest. The snacks on the tray were abundant and Steve imagined Maggie being generous to all her visitors. He scrutinised the contents more closely and of what appeared to be everything from coffee to tea, cake, biscuits and even packets of crisps. Maggie made space on the large low table which had engraved dragon heads on each corner.

'Before you start to ask me about my absent brother I will state that I have not seen nor heard from him since 1996,' said Maggie. 'He could be anywhere, even dead.'

'We understand that your late niece and her mother had lived with you a few years ago?' Julie asked.

'Yes it was rather dramatic the way it all happened,' Maggie paused, 'my brother had been brutal to Suwen more than once and her injuries were so awful.' She leant back into the sofa and crossed her legs, her long maxi skirt flapped elegantly each time she moved. 'I told all this to the previous detective…'

'We like to go over information again just in case something was missed,' Julie said, still not showing interest in the tray before her. 'Sara Li Eaton….' she said as she looked down at her note book, 'was Li her maiden name?'

'Her mother's Chinese name actually, so in a way yes. Sara was Chiwen Li Crawford…'

Steve suddenly sat forward at this name.

Maggie continued…'but decided to change her name by deed poll to Sara Li. She married Mark Eaton and became Sara Li Eaton.

'She divorced Mark Eaton a few months ago but kept his name,' Steve said.

'Much like me, I'm divorced too, but I kept my maiden name although I don't always use it…. only when I want to impress,' Maggie laughed.

'What is your impressing name now then,' Steve bantered.

'Mrs Crawford-Denning.'

Julie glanced at Steve who had become visibly restless. Maggie noticed this behaviour too.

'So where do you think her father had gone?'

'As I just said we never heard from him again, so I can't help not even to hazard a guess…' Maggie looked down then back up to Julie. 'Our parents disowned him. At one time he was doing so well in his studies, he was at medical school. Father stopped the fees and Lee had to leave and fend for himself…so God knows what he's done with his life since 1996.'

'I notice that you had not mentioned this to the previous detective?' Steve added.

'No, he didn't ask,' Maggie said with a shrug of her shoulders. Steve wondered if there could be a connection with the ITU doctor he'd met earlier in the week. This hunch prompted him to make a call to Moni. Julie smiled at his enthusiasm pleased he'd taken initiative to link evidence.

'My late niece could speak Mandarin, Chinese, as her mother was from China. Suwen taught Chi horoscopes with numbers but I don't think Chi fully grasped it. The two of them talked in Suwen's native language for hours…Chi, Sara, was very attentive to her mother you know, that photo on the sideboard was of the two of them before they moved here,' Maggie gave another sigh, 'she was such a sweet little girl, but she had changed dramatically, probably no thanks to her father.'

'Did you get on with Sara?' asked Julie.

'Well sort of, she was strange though, cold. She didn't even cry when her mother died. I suspect her death was a result of all her previous injuries.' She paused then leant forward as if to say something, then continued quietly as if in confidence, 'I'd go as far as to say she was hard, well to say she…lacked emotion…psychopathic tendencies perhaps…anyway I felt uncomfortable in her presence.' Maggie grimaced at the memory. 'Then …around that time she was accepted for nurse training. Hardly heard from her again,' she paused, 'it suited me really.'

'Are you familiar with psychiatric conditions?' Steve asked. Maggie sighed and looked at him and said.

'My ex-husband was a psychiatric nurse, he studied Sara's reaction to situations and his provisional diagnosis was that she showed signs of a psychiatric disorder. Probably due to trauma in childhood.... she had, seemed, to be bordering Asperger and appeared an obsessive compulsive disorder too, she constantly checked that everything was in a certain order and if moved or changed she would not get cross, instead she'd make sure it was back to how she had placed it. A little unnerving at times.'

An uncomfortable silence followed whilst coffee was poured. Steve took a piece of fruit cake and Julie smiled inwardly. All this new information was more than she could have imagined. Steve had already alerted Moni and hoped she would chase up their suspect's identity probably another person of interest she thought.

'Just one last question.... would you recognise your brother today?' asked Julie.

'Yes I think I would, even though it's been twenty years. At one time we had been close, until he went to private school in England.' Maggie went quiet in thought then she looked up at Julie. 'Do you think you know where my brother is?

Julie hesitated then said, 'Possibly.'

*

The drive back to Sussex took longer due to an accident on the M25 leaving confusion with traffic diversions and at rush hour time, too. The met office forecast a snow bomb, a latest terminology in weather, Steve imagined a giant snowball hurtling towards them, he told Julie which brought a smile to both the detectives' faces.

Back in the office Moni greeted them with a knowing smile something Julie liked to see, they were making headway at last. 'Well Moni?' Julie said, glued to the spot, 'What have you got?'

'Alan Clark admitted he was meeting Sara at the hospital to collect his personal items from her. They'd had a fling, his wife found out, drove off, got caught in a flood and drowned. Tragic outcome but he is now a suspect. He's detained downstairs.'

'Good work, and Dr Crawford?'

'Leonard Crawford,' Moni paused and consulted her notes, 'was at private school in England, parents lived in Hong Kong. Crawford married a Chinese national in 1984, was at med school in 1982 then later went back in 1996. His next of kin is Margret Crawford… his sister, don't know about his parents. Leonard Crawford now lives in Steyning - somewhere along the high street in one of those old three storey town houses.' Moni looked up and said, 'Plus Steve and I have already met him when we called on Dr Owen Muller.'

'Get him in Moni, take Steve with you….'

35

Maggie wasn't sure where the day surgery unit was so she asked at the outpatients book-in desk and one of the volunteers offered to take her there. It seemed safer to be taken there by a hospital representative rather than try to find it herself even though she had walked past the main door to this unit. The hospital was smaller than she remembered as chunks of it had been bulldozed to make way for a housing estate, losing the remainder of the hospital within it.

She thanked the outpatient volunteer. Knowing she would need to ask for the manager of the unit, she was pleased that she had phoned ahead to arrange this visit. Maggie wanted to see where the murder had taken place and wondered if the area would still be cordoned off to forensics. She walked around looking at the staff photos hanging on the wall, she studied each one but did not see one resembling her brother.... there was a gap where a photo had been removed which she wondered at perhaps a staff member that had left. She felt under scrutiny and took a quick look around her to see if anyone was watching her.

A nurse came back and took Maggie up to the first floor in a small lift big enough for a maximum of six people. It smelt of old plastic with the occasional whiff of bonfire smoke. Although only one floor up, it seemed to take ages and Maggie wondered if it would stop midway. As the lift door slowly slid open in a jerky movement Maggie found herself impatiently ready to squeeze herself out. The Manager was waiting in the reception area, her face deadly serious.

'My name is Emily, I'm the theatre manager,' she held out her hand to shake.

'Thank you for seeing me at such short notice.' Maggie shook hands with Emily.

'I'm so sorry…the detectives didn't say that you would be visiting, you've caught me on the hop really even though you phoned this morning.' Emily took a deep breath then sighed, and Maggie wasn't sure if it was out of relief or perhaps a little more notice would have left Emily better prepared.

'Is there anywhere more private where we could go rather than out here?' Maggie asked just as an operating trolley carrying an unconscious patient was pushed by slowly and because everyone seemed to be wearing the same theatre clothes, she assumed the person at the head would be the anaesthetist. The anaesthetist gave a quick glance over at Maggie, who stopped in mid-sentence her jaw dropped. It was her brother, an instant recognition - and she knew he'd spotted her too. His body language as he half turned again to glimpse her peripherally confirmed his recognition. She wondered if he would acknowledge her or perhaps come back. Once upon a time they were close and he would tell her his secrets. But she was not so sure he would share secrets now…. she sensed something sinister… her heart thumped so hard in her chest that she had to cough to calm it. No she was sure she didn't want to share his secrets this time…

Emily noticed this sudden interaction… and wondered what it was all about, perhaps Dr Crawford had anaesthetised her once or she knew him from elsewhere. Emily watched the distracted Maggie for a moment longer then said, 'Well I have an office which we could sit in…I'll make coffee for us there.' Without looking at Emily, the mesmerised Maggie said, 'No here will be okay…umm just for a while.'

In the background an unexpected influx of theatre staff congregated in the little kitchen area all squashed together just to make drinks. There was the sound of tin lids being removed and clanged down on the surface of the housekeeping trolley, and someone took out the assortment of cakes and laid them haphazardly on plates akin to a café or a scene at a fund raising even.

It was the sudden appearance of Lee's face framed by the small window of the recovery room door that startled Maggie. The two siblings looked at each other for a couple of minutes. It was more of a cold stare maybe because of the lapse of years or the fact his daughter was dead. The detective wanted him identified. She felt sick in the pit of her stomach. He disappeared and didn't return.

'I have a bad feeling about this…I think I'm going to be surprised at something?'

'Yes I think you may well be,' Maggie said uneasily, 'Is it ok to use my phone in the hospital?'

'Of course, you'll get a better signal in my office,' said Emily, sensing a change in Maggie's mood as tears glistened and Emily wondered if it was because Sara had died here, and perhaps the guilt of not keeping in contact. 'I'll leave your coffee on the desk.' Emily said.

As Maggie looked around the office she noticed how untidy it was, some documents had brown circles where mugs had been placed. She couldn't help thinking that had Sara been in here it would have been pristine tidy. She pushed the office door to, and keyed in Julie's mobile phone number from a police business card she was given earlier, it went into voice mail so she left a short message.

There was a commotion outside one of the theatres as it was being emptied of equipment, Maggie squinted a look through the narrow opening hoping to see her brother but it was hard to differentiate staff as they wore the same raspberry coloured overalls and blue hats. She thought of Sara once being part of this scene and felt her gaze drop, sad, her niece now dead, murdered. Maggie shuddered at the thought.

36

The late afternoon sun struggled to reach the high window and it gloomily peeped in through a network of grime. Steve hadn't noticed nature's attempt at the winter solstice and carried on sorting through the numbers that Sara had on her phone. They either meant or represented something and who they were for was only significant to her. Steve wondered that if this phone had been discovered earlier would it have solved the crime or been evidence of her killer or killers sooner.

It was good of Julie to let him research in her office undisturbed and he wanted to solve the puzzle himself so he could impress her, prove he was a good detective. Perhaps he was too eager to be noticed by the boss but he'd always wanted to be a detective and he knew he had the curiosity gene.

For Steve, the light bulb moment finally happened, could the numbers mean something in Chinese…a Chinese zodiac chart may help, along with the suspects dates of birth;, possible evidence, a connection?

He double checked the numbers from Sara's broken phone. The mysterious numbers on the phone boxes found earlier in Sara's house all linked in the phone contacts. Wondering if there was a connection, he googled a Chinese zodiac chart and scrolled to the years of the birth dates of the five men; each had an animal symbol, collection of lucky colours and numbers. Now all he needed was the date of birth of each suspect to prove his theory.

It had been an hour since Julie had left the office and she had her voice mail on, this always annoyed Steve, as he was eager to get some action. He looked through the photos again of Sara's mother at various stages of healing from her injuries. Why she had kept them remained a mystery.

Prior to her Death

The suspects dates of birts made sense with the zodiac charts right down to the animal symbols and they all linked in to the GPS tracking...so Sara could keep a tab on their whereabouts... he felt pleased with himself after all he had more pieces in the jigsaw.

37

Louise Brooks sat by her bedroom window watching the sparrows invade the bird table; good, she thought, she hated magpies and starlings, they were such bullies.

She heard her mother vacuuming downstairs. The sound of the Dyson seemed to change its volume and tone as it passed back and forth by the doors. Her mother could be so bossy at times so Louise preferred to stay up in her room until this part of the housework was done. She smiled to herself as she loved the status quo.

Louise switched on her iPhone pleased she'd got the GPS app on her phone and the fact she had managed to clone Sara's sim card made it easy. Immediately she spotted where Daniel was, hopefully with Liz. Then she traced the other phones, all innocuously going about their business, Owen at home, suspended from his job whilst this investigation was on going, David appeared to be at home doing what he does best, being a prat. No point in looking at Alan, he'd be at home moping and Louise doubted he'd carry that phone with him, so no point. Mark's phone never moved because he had simply discarded it.

She checked on Dr Leonard Crawford, Sara actually gave him a phone with a web site, containing photos, all very strange and suspicious to anyone. Louise had already seen them, quite nasty and gory. Who'd think a Consultant Anaesthetist could be so brutal to such a little woman, the bruises...oh God Sara's father, what a bastard, he needed to be punished for his past, she thought.

Blackmail was a good enough motive to murder someone, perhaps the police will think this because no one else would have such a strong motive, she cogitated. She checked to see where Dr Leonard Crawford was at that moment and was surprised to see he was in the operating theatre where Sara had been murdered! Great move Doc. In her excitement she phoned Julie to let her know...but Louise would have to give a convincing reason as how she knew he'd be there.

The CSSD driver was always collecting and returning equipment, Louise could say the driver saw Dr Crawford there and as he is friends with her, thought he'd let her know. No one would check the driver's comment as when they got to the hospital and found Dr Crawford, it would be end of story.... quite simple really.

38

The grey and lilac walls made the room feel cold. Lee wondered why tax payer's money couldn't have been put to better use with a more creative designer, perhaps a lemon and sandalwood combination, certainly a lot warmer. He thought of his late daughter Chi, how he had loved her and now his heart was broken at her loss. He started to cry again, something he thought he'd never do but for at births of his three children, Chi, Alex and Matilda. It would have been lovely to have his family complete at last.

The two detectives entered the interview room just as Lee blew his nose and wiped his eyes. They pulled out the plastic chairs from the under the table and sat themselves down. One of them turned on the recorder on the table and mumbled something into the recording device.

'Doctor Crawford you are under caution as you are helping us with our investigation.' Julie said. Steve sat quietly it was his boss's turn to ask questions.

'I understand that,' said Doctor Crawford wiping his now red, swollen eyes, though he tried so hard to keep the tears of grief back.

'Please give your name for the digital recorder, sir.'

'My name and details are, Doctor Leonard Crawford 11/01/1964. I reside at Down's House, High Street, Steyning, West Sussex.'

'Thank you…. now where were you on the night of the twenty ninth of November 2016?'

'Bordeaux France, I have a farm house there, I have witnesses to that effect.'

'Who would vouch for you being in France?' Julie asked.

'My wife, mother in law, Eurostar and the town's mayor. We dined with him on that night.'

'What was Sara Li Eaton to you?'

'My eldest daughter from my first marriage, her name was Chiwen Li Crawford.'

Julie instructed Steve to check the dates and venue for authenticity. It would mean contacting the French police to corroborate the town's mayor's movements that evening.

Without prompting Dr Crawford explained the recent connection with his daughter after twenty years.

'My marriage to Suwen had become intolerable, we married too young and were of two different cultures. My parents were right, it wouldn't work out.' He looked down as he paused, he put his hand up to his mouth, then said quietly, reflective of his actions, 'I just lost my temper, unusual for me but I had been pushed to my limit…. all over money…I thought she was saving our money and calculated we had over two grand. . ,' he started to shake his head then tears flowed as he said, 'she sent all that money to her mother to help her out of poverty, she told me as if it was the honourable thing to do.' Dr Crawford blew his nose as Julie and Steve looked on. 'I realised she'd put *us* into poverty instead, I was furious especially as she promised she'd never do it again…it worked out that, all told, four and a half grand had been sent over to her mother!'

Recognising his emotional state Julie said sympathetically. 'I think we'll take a break Dr Crawford, would you like a drink?' Julie didn't like to show too much of her soft side. The mood in the room felt quite charged with emotion, like after watching a heart-breaking movie. Julie thought of the scene from Titanic where all those dead bodies were bobbing around in the freezing Atlantic. It always got to her.

With the help of the extra detectives Dr Crawford's story was corroborated, and Julie wasn't surprised, he seemed genuine enough. Now that she had a free moment she could listen to her voice mail messages, one from Steve and his new discovery, she made a mental note to talk to him about that and a strange one from Louise Brooks.

Julie checked the time of the message and realised that Dr Crawford had been with them all morning. It couldn't be him at the scene of crime, so then who was it and how did Louise know?

Lee became more composed and it seemed that the coffee had hit the spot. The suicide note was inside an evidence bag and was handed carefully over to him. He held it in his hand and read it to himself. Julie noted he didn't need to wear glasses when reading and when he looked up at her she noted his dark almost emerald green eyes.

'It's thought to be a suicide note but of course other evidence points to murder,' said Julie, 'do you recognise this note?'

'Yes I'd sent it in an email to Chi, um…Sara, it was part of my explanation of what happened between her mother and me all those years ago.' He shook his head and put his hand up to his forehead like the great thinker, and he remained like that for a minute or so as tears dripped off his chin. He composed himself and blew his nose, his eyes were red from crying. 'Why would only part of the message be printed out and left with Chi…. ?'

'That is what we need to find out, but I will need to see the original email you had sent to Sara,' said Julie.

'I've got it on my iPhone, I could send it to you now and you can get it printed off yourself,' Lee said as he scrolled his phone to email and sent it to Julie. It took only a few seconds, which surprised Julie as often it can take a lot longer.

'Great I'll go and print it out now,' she said,' in the meantime Dr Crawford whilst we continue our investigation you are free to go but please do not leave the area as we may need to speak to you again soon.' Julie paused and as if in thought said, 'Do you have that spare phone your daughter gave you?'

'Yes but it's locked in the anaesthetic cupboard in theatre two at Southlands Hospital.

After seeing the photos I told Sara that when I got back from France we'd have plenty of time to catch up and I would explain what happened.' Lee said rubbing his slightly bristly chin. 'I wanted her to meet my new family, her new family, at some point, her half sister and brother.' As he shook his head tears splattered over his trouser. He was a broken man.

*

One of the female civilian staff had just finished on the phone and turned to Steve and said.

'A Jim Crosby says he has found a strange face on one of his photos that he took when he was up in the theatre on the night of the murder,' she said. 'I told him to bring his phone in to show you, Steve.'

'He didn't mention this to me at interview...why did he take a photo that night?' Steve asked looking confused.

'He said he took a photo of the flashing light in the control panel as he thought he might not remember which light it was,' the staff member said, 'then he suddenly remembered and took a look at which light it was and saw a face looking at him through the gap in the door. He felt the place was spooked with a ghost as he had a strange shift that night and that maybe he was looking a ghost in the eyes!' the amused staff member said.

*

Julie perched herself on the edge of Moni's desk tapping her teeth with a dry marker pen whilst staring at the incident board clearly in deep thought. 'Right gather round,' Julie said as she took a sweeping glance at her team from over her shoulder. 'I find it incredible that all our suspects have alibis and motives, there's no evidence to prove they were involved with the demise of Sara Eaton.' She stood and walked over to the board and changed the photos around. This time she put all the suspects' photos around in a circle with nothing in the middle, and pointing to the space she said, 'that's who murdered Sara Eaton.' She put a question mark in the space. The team look quizzically at one another as Steve removed a photo from an envelope in the internal mail.

'I've had this photo blown up by our tech team,' Steve said as he turned it around in his hand to show Julie, 'it looks familiar?' Julie studied it carefully and looked up at Steve.

'Who took this photo?'

'The night housekeeper.' Steve said.

'Why?'

'Well it was of the bleeping gas alarm, he didn't understand it so he took a photo of its screen to show to his supervisor, not noticing the face at the time.'

'What date and time was this taken?' Julie asked.

'Twenty ninth November at twenty fifty hundred hours.'

'Okay Steve, let's go.' Julie said.

The sudden noise of scraping chairs was like a chorus of screeching seagulls as staff moved to and from their desks. Some of them followed Julie and Steve as back up.

39

Julie rang the doorbell, and Mrs Brooks answered it with her cheery smile. Louise was curious and came down stairs to see who it was and found two detectives standing in the hall, when her mother, about to say something. Louise looked down at the phone she had in her hand then quickly shoved it into the back pocket of her jeans.

'We have a few more questions for you,' said Julie, as Steve took a step forward.

'May I have your phone please,' asked Steve, with his hand outstretched.

'What on earth for...what do you want?' Louise said as her eyes went from one detective to the other.

'We have reason to believe you have had access to Sara Eaton's sim card from her iPhone.'

'What?' Louise over- reacted as she took a step back. Slowly she took the phone from her back pocket and reluctantly handed it over to Steve. There was no passcode so he accessed the phone with ease as he scrolled the numbers in the phone book. Louise looked away from her mother who quietly stood by listening.

'These numbers you have on your phone are the same as the numbers found in Sara Eaton's home. Also I notice you have a tracking device on these numbers much like the app Sarah had on her iPhone?' Steve said as he studied the list of numbers that Julie had given him, 'ah… two and number three, that matches Dr Crawford, numbers one, six, and seven match, Dr Muller, David Lewis, Alan Clark and Daniel Franks - all their numbers match the list.'

'Why do you have their numbers on your phone?' asked Julie.

'There's no law saying I can't have numbers in my contacts,' the worried looking Louise said, as she ran her tongue around her lips

Well actually they match with Sara Eaton's numbers too. Why are you following their whereabouts?' Julie said, 'It appears that two three is at the hospital, you said that Dr Crawford was there and that you were informed by a delivery personnel?' Julie said looking intently at Louise. 'I put it to you Louise that you had been monitoring these men and now you're trying to put the blame on her father Dr Crawford who was not at the hospital this morning, by the way, but had left his phone locked in a cupboard there,' Julie said.

'This doesn't prove I murdered her…' Louise said with a smirk.

'I didn't say you did,' said Julie, 'Where were you on the night of the twenty ninth of November?'

'Here with my mother.' Louise looked at her mother for support but this time she looked away and shook her head.

'You went out after dinner Louise, for about an hour or so and came back around nine,' her mother said emphatically as she wiped tears from her eyes.

'We note that you declined a swab for your DNA?'

'Yes.' said Louise.

'We will need it now as you have become a suspect,' Julie said, 'and we need to eliminate you.' Louise looked indifferent, it was hard to read her emotion. 'Also we need to search your house, computer paper and printer, we can get a warrant if you prefer.'

'Come back tomorrow and you can search then!' Louise blurted.

Prior to her Death

'Ok, but in the meantime we need you to accompany us to the station for further questioning,' Julie gave her a hard stare and said, 'We have a witness that saw you at the hospital at twenty fifty hundred hours on the twenty ninth of November and later after you had abandoned or murdered Sara, you left your theatre shoes kicked off in the middle of the staff room.'

No one spoke, it was a typical response of being given bad news, never a nice moment, waiting for someone to cry or collapse, Julie thought. The two detectives remained still, waiting for some kind of reaction from Louise.

'Prove it.' she said calmly.

Steve showed Louise the photo that the night housekeeper had taken of the alarm panel where Louise was looking straight at the camera through the gap of the theatre door that was ajar because of a wedge. 'On your theatre shoes are the initial, EB, Elouise Brooks. The housekeeper had already cleaned the shoes in the female changing room and found yours kicked off in the middle of the floor, later.' There was a deathly hush as would be found in a mortuary. In the background, Louise's TV was blaring out adverts whilst steam puffed through from the kitchen where her mother had been bringing vegetables to boil, lids chattering under the pressure. An occasional whiff of roast pork permeated the hall and reached the nostrils of both detectives who at that moment listened to their own stomachs groaning for food.

'There's also another matter, we believe you copied Sara Eaton's numbers and started your own tracking of these men, one in particular you were trying to frame for the murder. But his phone had been kept locked in a cupboard in theatre two, the reason why it never moved.

'The identification numbers to each phone contact represented the suspects' birth dates in Chinese,' Steve proudly said, as Julie issued the arresting statement…

'Louise Brooks I'm arresting you for the murder of Sara Eaton, anything you ….. .'

*

Later the next day the team met up in the local pub to celebrate their result. Defoe popped in for a quick celebratory drink. 'There, I knew I could rely on you all, great team work, well done…now I suppose I'd better drink up and let you lot get on with your…party!' He downed his drink in one and left them all to it.

'It seems that Louise had cloned the sim, gained access to the contacts and probably used some sort of software to put a tracker on the other phones. Too smart for her own good,' said Steve proudly as now he felt he had been accepted into the MCT. He was one of the team.

Acknowledgements.

I'd like to give a huge thank you to the following people who helped with research for this story, along with their advice, constant encouragement and interest throughout.

Georgina Edge; Peter James; Steve Roberson; Sandra Roberson; Heidi McCall; Joe Bullingham;

Brendon Glynn; Rebecca Seymour; Mathew Bridle; Georgie Campsey; Louise Hardman and Sandra Hardman.

And to anyone that I missed out, you know who you are!

About the Author

Kathy Bullingham was born in the United Kingdom in 1950 where she lives with her husband. She is a retired nurse who had articles published in the Nursing press. This is her first attempt at a murder mystery novel.
